New Gun in Town

In a blur of action, Bide Evans slapped his holsters and tipped back his chair.

The dining room split wide open with the crash and roar of six-guns, and the acrid odor of black powder swirled through the room in blue-white streamers.

As he went over backward, the Texan set up a murderous crossfire, laying his left-hand gun under his right and letting it run red toward the man at the center table; in the meantime holding his bucking right-hand gun in a straight bead on the tall hombre . . .

The SHERIFF of HANGMAN'S GULCH

by

MATT RAND

WILDSIDE PRESS

1. Night Attack

Joe Hale, lank, taciturn placer miner, put his heft against the boulder and heaved. It toppled with sudden swiftness, and crashed with a loud swish into the stream. Small geysers caught rainbows from the setting sun.

Wiping the sweat off his forehead, Hale set to work with pick and shovel. In flood season, the boulder had been submerged by the stream, and the top gravel the miner now shoveled aside was still damp.

"How's it comin', Joe?" called Bill Clayson, Hale's curly-haired, stumpy partner, from a dozen feet away at the edge of the stream.

Clayson sat beside a four-foot cradle-shaped trough that stood on two rockers, one a few inches higher than the other, and was rolling it from side to side. With his free hand he scooped water from the stream with a tin dipper and kept pouring it into the open box at the high end of the trough. Sediment sifted out of the lower end.

Hale merely nodded as he swung the pickaxe. He went down to hardpan and then with the shovel, lifted the loosened dirt into a bucket at his feet. He left off and came over to the trough. Clayson watched him empty the bucket into the box at the upper end.

"The hopper needs fixin', Bill," Hale said, pointing to a loose corner on the box.

"So does yore disposition, Joe," cried his partner, working again with the dipper. "So tomorrer night we go to town to celebrate."

"Celebrate what?" demanded Hale dubiously.

"Why yuh old skinflint," cried Clayson with mock seriousness, "didn't this beautiful, little rocker—" he patted the trough, "—give us six pounds of gold dust this week? And look at them cleats." He unhinged the hopper, swung it up to a point at the bottom of the rocker, into which traverse riffle cleats had been driven. Fine, dull,

5

yellow flakes clustered around them. He let the hopper fall back into place and looked up, smiling. "We must've taken out close to two pounds more today, Joe—and the bar ain't begun to be worked yet."

" 'Bout time," said Hale, his dour expression brightening. "Took us a year to find it. Wish there was a bank in town we could keep the dust in," he added.

"Larson offered us the use of his safe," said Clayson, continuing to dip water and roll the rocker. "Said everyone uses it."

"Maybe we will go into town tomorrer—and leave our gold with Larson," said Hale.

"He didn't worry yuh with his talk of Black Henry and the Hounds—did he?" demanded Clayson.

"Maybe so," admitted Hale.

"No claim-jumpin' hyena is goin' to take this piece of pay dirt away from us," cried Clayson pugnaciously. Then he laughed. "Heck, Joe," he said. "Let's not get to fightin' shadders. " 'Sides—" and he tapped the gun holstered at his thigh.

Joe Hale shrugged his bony shoulders and returned to the digging. The two men worked steadily until dusk, then knocked off. Night fell by the time they collected the settlings that had gathered around the cleats in the rocker. These were transferred to a milkpan and dried over a fire. Then the hot sand was blown away, leaving the gold.

Bill Clayson brought out a small pouch made of cowhide and poured the gold from the pan into it. He restored the bag to his shirt.

The two partners, fatigued from a full day's work, went through a meal of hardtack, jerky and some coffee. They dozed a while around the fire, then rolled into their blankets—blissfully unaware that cruel, rodent eyes watched their every move. Gradually, the fire faded to a ruddy char.

The murderous raid came without warning, and the two partners never had a chance. A half dozen black-clad men charged suddenly into the camp, yelling hideous screams, unloosing a withering blast of gunfire upon the blanket-swathed, sleeping men.

Bill Clayson awoke, clutching his gun. "Black Henry—the Hounds!" he howled, catching sight of the ominous figures etched against the late moon. On his knees, he

6

triggered his Colt as the tide of death swooped down on him.

Then a crushing, ripping blow crashed against Clayson's brain and the universe seemed to explode in his face. He toppled and lay senseless.

His partner never moved from his blanket; never woke. He died in his sleep. A lucky man, Joe Hale.

The leader of the raiders, a huge, hulking figure in the night, kicked up the embers of the dying fire. Sparks and a dull glow temporarily lighted the damp. He stooped over Clayson's prone form, rifled his pockets and came out with the cowhide pouch. He grunted with satisfaction.

"Take these two gents downstream, where it's plenty deep," he ordered his men. "Tie a heavy rock to their bodies, and throw 'em in."

Four men moved to obey and soon trundled the dead men out of camp. The fifth spoke to the leader.

"How 'bout their tools, Black Henry?" he asked. "Get rid of 'em?"

"No," grunted the big man. "This claim'll be worked tomorrer. Yuh head back to the cabin, Lem. Tell the boys I went to town. Be back later."

Several miles from the scene of sudden death in a miner's camp, two men sat. For a time, a brittle silence lay between them; then it splintered in the voice of one.

"Wearin' them fancy pants and clothes ain't rubbed the smell of wolf off yuh, Jim."

"Yuh wore fancy pants once, Matt. Remember?" he asked softly.

A chair scraped against the wall somewhere in the dark. "Don't remind me of that!" The voice was harsh, bitter, and slightly thickened with drink.

"All right, Matt," the man called Jim said. "But don't forget these clothes made me a good and respected citizen of Hangman's Gulch." He laughed again.

"But not respectable enough to get yuh Kate Larson—huh, Jim?" he taunted.

Jim's laugh died in his throat. He banged his fist down on the table. The whiskey glass jumped. Amber-colored liquor spilled over its edge and made a thin, glistening streak on the wood.

"I'll get her," he cried, his face glowing curiously in the yellow light.

7

During the day, Jim Wurt looked like the aggressive, reputable businessman that he appeared to be.

Yet somehow, a darkened room and candlelight brought into relief his dominant features; his hooked nose, his high, pale forehead, his black glittering eyes—and made him somehow sinister-looking. In his unguarded moments, despite the white linen shirt and black frock coat of respectability, Jim Wurt had the look of a man who ran with the wolf pack—at its head—as lobo wolf.

"Yuh ain't forgettin' Sam Larson, are yuh, Jim?" drawled Matt.

Jim Wurt's face mottled. "Blast him," he cried. "He thinks his daughter's too good for me." He laughed harshly. "But honest Sam Larson's due for a surprise one of these days. And mighty soon, too." His tone changed and interest ruffled it. "Weren't yuh soft on her when yuh fresh came here?"

"Changed my mind!" said Matt abruptly. Drink slowed his voice, thickened it. "Don't forget that Sam Larson's a powerful man in this here town. Judge Carter's his best friend; Sheriff Sears; the whole Vigilante Committee—"

"The whole Committee except one, Matt," replied Wurt, smiling, restored to good humor. "Me—Number Eight."

"I got to hand it to yuh, Jim," admitted Matt. "Yuh sure pulled a whizzer on 'em."

"Make that present and future," said Wurt, "and yuh'll be right."

Matt's short laugh had sarcasm in it. "Yuh're right proud of yoreself, ain't yuh, Jim? Don't forget what the Good Book says. 'Pride goes before a fall.'" He chuckled thickly. "Bet the good folk of the Gulch would be kind of surprised to learn that Jim Wurt kept just one step ahead of the law in Texas. The sheriff—blast him—suspected Mr. Wurt of changin' brands, but never got a chance to prove it—'cause Mr. Wurt skipped Texas and came to California to become a respectable saloon owner—"

"Shut up, Matt!" snapped Wurt, anger flushing his high forehead.

"Sorry, Jim," mumbled Matt. "Forgot. Sorry." But liquor had loosened his tongue, and he rambled on. "Was a good idea, buyin' this saloon. But it sure gets me how yuh won enough playin' poker to do it. Yuh was always an easy trim—"

8

The door across the room suddenly creaked open. For a brief instant, a huge, shapeless hulk of a man stood on the threshold—outlined by a distant dim light of the sleeping town. The newcomer quickly shut the door, strode to the table, lifted the filled whiskey glass and tossed the drink down.

He took a chair and sat down; but kept his face well beyond the flickering range of the candle. Jim Wurt's nocturnal visitors invariably kept to the shadows. Only the newcomer's hands, huge and hairy, showed against his black trousers.

"Well?" Wurt was standing expectantly. On his feet, the saloon-owner was not a tall man.

In answer, the man tossed a small, cowhide pouch onto the table. It struck the boards with a heavy *thwut*.

Avidly, Wurt seized it up, pulled open the drawstring and tilted the bag's mouth into his hand. A small stream of dull yellow metal flakes, grains and kernels sifted out. Cold glitter burned in his black eyes.

"This is sure gettin' monotonous." It was Matt's drawling, thickened voice from the wall. "Say, Black Henry—how much did that there gold dust cost the state of California?"

The big man—Black Henry—laughed coarsely. "Two prospectors," he answered.

Disgust crowded Matt's voice. "Yuh're a cold-blooded killer—ain't yuh?"

"Why yuh onery—" began Black Henry, and his chair scraped in the darkness.

"Keep quiet, yuh two!" hissed Wurt, looking up. "Want to wake up the whole town?"

Black Henry eased off. "Some day, friend," he growled to his tormentor, "yuh're goin' to push them jokes too far."

"It ain't the jokes I'm waitin' to push far," grunted the blear-eyed, stubble-faced man against the wall.

Jim Wurt had gone under the table to fetch a scale and some weights, and was now weighing the gold. Once more he turned to his two henchmen, his black eyebrows bristling.

"Listen," he grated angrily. "As long as I'm bossin' the outfit, I don't want any arguments—understand? Matt—Black Henry?" Both men subsided in the darkness. Wurt went back to the scales; adjusted the weights carefully. "Eight pounds," he finally announced with satisfaction.

He placed the gold pouch into an inner pocket and extracted a large wad of bills. He counted some out and handed them to Black Henry. "One thousand dollars," he said. "Fifty percent—accordin' to our agreement."

Black Henry handled the bills carefully, his huge hands deft in the shuffling. "Right," he said, pocketing the money. "Send yore man out to the cabin tomorrer mornin' and I'll have one of the boys show him the bar."

Nodding, Wurt handed Black Henry a folded slip of paper. "Entered today," he said.

The chair tilted against the wall thudded down softly; and the tall, unsteady form of Matt showed faintly in the dull light.

"Gentlemen," he said, his tongue rolling, "I'm gettin' mighty tired of not bein' a millionaire. How 'bout stakin' out one of them claims for me?"

"Maybe I'll do that for yuh soon, pard," growled Black Henry. "A nice, rich diggin'."

Matt laughed thickly. "We'll work that one together, friend." He turned and made his way out.

"One day I'm goin' to cut out his heart," rasped Black Henry.

Wurt considered the black, shapeless form in the shadows, his eyes reflective. "Better go slow," he said casually. "There's only one hombre I ever saw faster than Matt on the draw—" his face clouded, "—and that ain't yuh. 'Sides, he rides herd over my town crew."

"Why do yuh let him drink so much?" asked the other.

"His wife died some time back," replied Wurt. "He forgets when he drinks—and it keeps him out of serious trouble. Anyhow I got an idea in back of my head, and Matt's the hombre to handle it." His voice fell almost to a whisper, and his eyes showed bright and shiny in the candlelight: "An idea that'll put Hangman's Gulch into my back pocket."

"What's yore idea, Wurt?" demanded Black Henry, interest thick in his voice.

The glance the saloon owner swung at his henchman was void of expression. "My agreement with yuh," he said coldly, "covers only the claims—that's all. Any other, er—enterprises I engage in, are exclusively mine. *Sabe?*"

"Sure." The big, hairy hands of Black Henry disappeared as he pushed his chair back and rose. He moved to the door.

"Oh yeah," said Wurt casually. "I want to make a bet with yuh, Black Henry."

"Bet?" The floor boards creaked as the big man turned.

"Yeah," replied Wurt. "A thousand dollars against yore hundred the new sheriff's still alive in forty-eight hours."

Black Henry snorted. "It's a bet."

The door opened and shut. And the room was empty, save for frock-coated Jim Wurt, respectable saloon owner. For a moment his eyes had a faraway look. Then he fetched the cowhide pouch from his pocket, opened its throat and poured the yellow stream into his hand. A quiet, pleasant smile came to his face as he played with the gold.

2. *Hangman's Gulch*

HANGMAN'S GULCH lay somnolent in the tawny light of the morning. And morning's stillness ran the length of the empty, sun-baked main stem.

Once, the town was a brush-choked, stream-cleft gorge whose brown-earth slopes were covered with pines and oak. That had been a long time ago—as Californians reckoned time. But no more than two years in anyone else's calendar.

Two fateful years had passed since James Marshall rushed nervously from the mill on the Columa to Sutter's Fort to tell John Sutter of his great, secret discovery. A secret that was impossible to keep, and soon caught up by a trembling, feverish nation, and flung to the four corners of the earth.

Two years since the first faint trickle of gold-seekers from the Midwest "saw the elephant" on the way across Truckee Pass, high in the icy Sierras; since the first ship from the east, from the European Continent, from Asia—from the seven seas, dumped their human cargoes on San Francisco's windy, foggy beach.

Clapboard towns sprang up to serve the needs of this horde of miners. Half the buildings were used as gambling houses, saloons and hotels. Merchants and vendors held the rest.

It was inevitable that the nation's riffraff should follow in the wake of the gold-seekers. Slit-eyed, gun-heeled men, they came separately, or in pairs—and like filings attracted to a magnet, banded together to prey upon miner and merchant alike.

And it was a lucrative field for the development of their peculiar talents. For despite the fact that California early became a state, law and order were merely unconfirmed rumors in many communities.

Tough killers walked the streets; bold robberies went unchecked, and claim-jumping became an everyday occurrence.

To challenge this wave of terror and crime, honest townfolk banded together into Vigilante Committees, held trials and dispensed justice. Armed, deadly conflict raged between the two forces. Blood was spilled, lives lost.

Hangman's Gulch was typical of the times; and no exception to the bloody strife that ransacked the countryside.

A prospector had found gold in the stream that bisected the Gulch, and soon a town grew on a bottom where only brush and tough yucca had grown before.

Out of the morning, a man reeled and staggered into the outskirts of Hangman's Gulch. The early summer sun, yellow on the trail, was ghastly on the man's face. Dried blood matted his curly hair and clung in grisly, jagged streaks to his flushed cheeks. His eyes were glazed and feverish; his lips cracked, bleeding.

His black suit, dirt-smeared, torn, lay stiff against him. And bullet holes showed round, purple patches at his shoulder and chest and thigh.

As he lurched along, babbling sounds issued from his mouth, and spittle flecked his stubbled chin. Then suddenly, he plunged into the street and lay in an inert heap, while the dust he had disturbed settled down slowly over him in a brown, yellowish cloud.

In a few moments a small, somber-faced crowd had gathered around the unconscious man. Then they made way for Judge Carter and Sam Larson, who edged through the crowd. "Get some water, someone," called the lat-

12

ter, as he went down on his knees beside the sprawled miner.

Sam Larson was the richest but best-liked man in the Gulch. There was not a man in that crowd who hadn't owed him money at one time or another, and who had been reminded of that debt.

Someone thrust a water canteen into Larson's hand. He cradled the miner's head in his elbow and forced the snout into the man's mouth. Water trickled out on the insensible man's chin.

Larson shook his head dubiously at the judge.

"Who is he, Sam?" asked the latter. Artemus Carter, the Gulch's first judge, was a trim figure of a man in his black frock coat and flowing black bowtie. A silvered goatee and clear blue eyes dominated his face. In court the judge was highly impartial and considered himself but an instrument of the law.

"Think his name is Clayson—Bill Clayson," replied Larson slowly, frowning. "Yeah. He and his pard bought some supplies at the store 'bout ten days ago. Then he came back and filed a claim—"

A moan slipped past the lips of the dying man. And pain contorted his blood-streaked face. He stirred, then his eyes fluttered weakly open. They were bleary, glazed; held no recognition.

Again Larson spilled water into the miner's mouth. "How'd it happen, friend?" he asked.

For an instant, comprehension flashed across Clayson's face and his battered lips tried to form words. Mumbled sounds came from his mouth. His ravaged cheeks flexed, and heavy sweat beaded his forehead. But the struggle was in vain. One word that sounded like "Henry," came past Clayson's lips—and he gave up the fight.

Then death claimed Bill Clayson and his mouth fell open and his eyes stared sightless at the blue sky.

Sam Larson rose slowly, his glance touching the crowd, then coming to rest on a man there. "Harvey," he said. "Take care of Clayson. I'll stand the burial."

Faces grave, Sam Larson and Judge Carter walked down the street in silence. A third man, a latecomer to the scene, swung in beside them.

"What happened?" he asked.

Tay Brown was a dark-humored man with a steady stare and a bullet scar red along his jaw. Across the

13

gambling table once, an ugly customer had called Brown a "cheat." That was the first and last time anyone ever called him that. He wore that scar as a flaming signal to the world; for Tay Brown was known and respected as a "square" gambler.

The two men nodded to him and the judge told him briefly what had occurred.

"Black Henry!" cried the gambler.

"Yeah—damn his hide," cried Larson angrily.

The judge interrupted. "We can't be certain it is Black Henry, Sam. All Clayson mumbled before he died was 'Henry.' It may have been his son, or partner—or anybody."

The general store owner shook his shaggy head violently. "It's that murderin' coyote and his gang of hoodlums—and no one else. Yuh know it, Judge, and I know it—and so does every one in the Gulch! They're responsible for every claim-jump and killin' in the last four months."

It was the judge's turn to shake his head. "Insufficient evidence, Sam," he said. "No one saw Black Henry commit this crime. All you have is a corpus delicti—that's all. It won't stand up in court. You'll need more than that to convict Black Henry."

Sam Larson swore underneath his breath. "Insufficient evidence! That's always the trouble," he cried irately. "If we get a witness against him—he dies. Or else we get someone who's afraid to talk—"

"Can't blame 'em, Larson," declared Tay Brown. "Their hides wouldn't be worth an ounce of dust if they did."

Larson turned on him, eyes flashing. "That ain't a way to talk, Brown," he declared. "If no one spoke up, we'd have no law and order—"

"We don't have much anyhow," said the gambler, flushing.

"If we get rid of Black Henry," cried Larson, "we will."

"In the meantime," said Brown, "he comes to town when he pleases and walks the streets free and easy."

"The time for that will soon be over," declared Sam Larson. "We're goin' to—"

Judge Carter interrupted sternly: "Don't tell me about your Committee of Vigilantes, Sam. It's extralegal—outside the law. I won't countenance its actions, nor do I want to hear of it."

"Yuh can't lock yoreself up behind stone walls, Judge," cried Brown, "and say there ain't no wind howlin' outside, when everybody hears a storm. Black Henry's a menace to the folk in the Gulch—and if the law won't take care of him, the Vigilantes will."

"If Black Henry breaks the law," said the judge gruffly, "the sheriff will apprehend him and bring him to trial. Otherwise, and until such evidence is produced which will prove him guilty in court, Black Henry is free to come and go as he pleases."

"Tom Sears is a good sheriff," declared Larson. "But he's up against somethin' here that's just too big for one man to handle."

"The sheriff possesses the right to deputize as many men as he deems necessary," said the judge. "If Sears needs help, he knows what to do about it."

"That ain't the point, Carter," cried Larson. "Yuh know a man with a star pinned to his vest makes him an easy target. That's why we organized the Committee—" He broke off abruptly and his wide mouth snapped shut.

By now the three men had reached Larson's store. A man had just come out, and it was his appearance that caused the store owner's face to grow grim and stormy.

Jim Wurt was dressed meticulously and his face shone from a recent shave.

"Good mornin', gentlemen," he said pleasantly, his wet, red lips receding in a smile.

"Is my daughter inside?" demanded Larson curtly, scarcely acknowledging the greeting.

"Yeah," replied Wurt, the edge rubbing off his smile. "She asked me to send yuh in."

"Wurt," cried Larson, his face working red. "I told yuh twice before to stay away from Kate. This is the last time—and this is a warnin'!"

Judge Carter laid a restraining hand on the big-boned storekeeper, but the latter shook it off.

"I know yuh don't like me, Larson," Wurt said. "And I ain't aimin' to start any arguments—this mornin'. But I reckon it's up to Miss Larson to tell me that herself."

No one knows what would have happened next if a horse hadn't suddenly broken into town and flashed down the street, kicking up a swirling dust cloud. A sense of urgency sat in the rider's saddle.

The sweat-lathered horse brought up on its haunches as the rider came sailing off in front of the four men. He was a lad of no more than fourteen.

"What's the rush, Bud?" demanded Brown.

The youngster stood in front of them panting, his face worried, his eyes big and round.

"I just cut Sheriff Sears down," he cried. "He was hangin' from a tree—about two miles out of town. And his badge was missin'." With that, the youngster turned heel and ran into the store two removed from Larson's. The legend painted on the window was, "Dan River's Printing Shop." Underneath that appeared the words, "Hangman's Gulch *Weekly Herald*."

Consternation, then anger showed on honest Sam Larson's face. "Murdered!" he cried fiercely. "First West and now Sears! This is Black Henry's bloody work!"

"There's no proof yet," said the judge temperately.

"Enough for me, Carter—and the Committee," cried Larson. "Tom told me yesterday he was on that big devil's trail. Said Black Henry and the Hounds had a cabin in the hills 'round here."

"What'll we do about a sheriff," asked Wurt quietly, "to take Sears' place?"

"There'll be an election," announced the judge. "As the law prescribes."

"That'll take two weeks," pointed out Tay Brown.

"The law may move slowly, gentlemen," said the judge. "But it moves. I'm going to have Rivers make the announcement in his paper." He nodded, and moved with unhurried and dignified stride to the store where the *Herald* was printed.

"He'll never learn," cried Larson bitterly. He turned grimly to Brown. "But we ain't waitin' for no election. I'm callin' a meetin' of the Committee for tonight." His glance reluctantly included Jim Wurt.

"I'll be there," said Wurt. He smiled pleasantly and left them.

"Can't understand what yuh have against Jim Wurt," said Brown.

Larson's wide mouth drew in as he watched Wurt disappear into the Star Saloon. "I can't put my finger on it, Brown," he said unsmiling. "But there's somethin' in

16

that gent I don't trust. Maybe it's because that bunch of hoodlums uses Wurt's place to meet."

"I think yuh got him figgered wrong, Larson," declared Brown, shaking his head. "Business is business, 'sides there's never been a suspicion on him. Why he's Number Eight."

Two meetings took place that night—not one. And the latter meeting was a counterpart of one that had taken place on many previous occasions—in the single, candle-lighted back room of the Star.

Black Henry had just let his bulk in quietly through the door and taken his seat. Wurt's face glowed sepulchrally in the yellow light as he finished counting some money from a roll of bills.

"Guess I lost that bet, huh?" he said smiling.

Black Henry's coarse laughter rumbled low in the room. "That'll learn yuh not make any more dumb fool bets with me." A hairy hand broke into the dimly lit circle and took the money Wurt had extended. Then the hands' owner said, "Brought yuh a present, Wurt." And an object was thrown cnto the table.

For a moment, Jim Wurt stared at it; then a smile brushed his full lips. And he picked the shiny object up and slipped it into his pocket.

"That'll hang yuh, friend," Matt's taunting voice floated thickly from the wall, where he had his chair tipped.

"Sure," laughed Black Henry. "Right beside yuh."

"Let up, yuh two," said Wurt, but it was evident that he was in a good humor. "And listen to me."

Silence descended over the glimmering darkness of the room. Silence broken only by the softly pushing voice of Jim Wurt, weaving a web of chicanery and cunning.

Once Matt objected. "But Texas—" he began.

Wurt cut him off. "Texas is a lcng way from here," he said. "And as long as yuh're workin' for me—" he shrugged.

The candle sputtered, neared the nadir of its descent. Still the purring voice went on. Finally Wurt reached the end.

"And Black Henry," he concluded, "my brother members on the Vigilante Committee are goin' to comb the woods for yuh. Just disappear for a week." Then he sent his voice reaching to Matt in the darkness. "And remember, Matt. We remain strangers to each other—the way we been—'til this business is settled. Then we'll see how the play falls."

When he had done, his two henchmen joined him in a drink; then the three plotters departed separately, and in silence.

3. Claim-Jumpers

THE LONG-LEGGED black made it up the sharp, rugged scarp and stood blowing and heaving on the patchy crest. The late afternoon sun, still warm, came out of the western fringe of hills to greet the lone rider, and splayed him with flat, yellow sunshine.

Bide Evans flung his hand up against the glare. He blinked as his eyes pierced the faded western distance and found faint smoke curling skyward from vague rooftop shapes. He nodded slightly.

"Reckon that's Hangman's Gulch, mister—the last stop down the line." Evans spoke to his horse, as men do when they ride the range or trail alone. "Six months," he muttered bitterly. "Six months—and nary a sign."

The bitterness in his voice lay reflected in the ingrown canker of his deep-set gray eyes. And in the lines of his face that pulled his lips together, tight and thin. Yet his eyes had not always been bitter in his twenty-five years.

It was a strong face, where bitterness and determination sat evenly matched. It was lean of shank, but square of chin—a chin covered with thick, barbed-wire stubble, red in color. As brick red as the tangle of hair that lay thatched underneath his Stetson.

"From Truckee Pass to Frisco," he muttered grimly. "From Mt. Shasta all the way down here, to Hangman's Gulch—and nary a trace of him—nary a sign." He shook his head stubbornly. "He must be in California. He was seen comin' through the pass."

He shrugged his wide shoulders, and spoke again to his black: "But we ain't found him, mister. Reckon that means we'll be headin' for home tomorrer."

18

Then, for perhaps the hundredth time since he had received it back in San Francisco, he drew a letter from his breast pocket.

He knew the contents as he did the back of his hand. Yet every time he read it, his throat choked him and anger raked him like a fiery brand. He hadn't shaved since he had received it. The letter was brief and said:

Dear Bide,

Your mother died shortly after you left—of a broken heart. Come back to Texas, son, and the Circle E. I'm getting old and weary, and the spread needs you to ramrod it.

We're a proud family, Bide—maybe too proud. That's why I'm asking you to leave off and come home. Your mother would have wanted it that way, too.

Your Father.

Bitterness lay across his face like an open wound. His mother dead, and his father bending under the strain. All because of—

He stuffed the letter back into his pocket. Yes, he thought grimly, they had been a proud family. Proud and stubborn. That's why he had clung to the trail until now. That's why he had written back that he would stay it to the end.

But Hangman's Gulch was the end. It was the last mining town down the line. Only a dogged presistence had kept him going this far. Even to himself he had been unwilling to acknowledge its futility. But he recognized it now. It was all over. Maybe it was best that way? *Quien sabe?*

At any rate, he had ridden the hot sun from mining camp to mining camp the whole day—as he had these past six months. And he had broken cold camp this morning, therefore the prospect of a hot bath and a good meal at Hangman's Gulch, was inviting. So the redheaded Texan kneed his mount forward; and the animal went down the slope.

The black had shifted into an easy walk and soon neared stream level. Evans' ears became filled with the sound of rushing water. That's why he did not hear the clump of shovel biting into earth and the hoarse growl of

19

low-pitched voices, until his mount sidled around a small tree cluster. Then he pulled to an abrupt halt.

A curious piece of business was going on here. A man was engaged in digging a shallow ditch, about six feet long, while five others stood around and watched—silently, and somehow sinisterly.

These were gun-heeled men dressed alike in black. And it was their horses, evidently, that stood bunched at the other end of the clearing, near a lean-to.

There was an ominous note about the proceedings that caused Evans to slip silently out of leather and glide unnoticed into the shadow of a tree trunk. In the quick glance he looped around the camp, he recognized here a dry diggings. Two buckets stood near fresh-turned earth on the rocky hillside. And down near the clay cut-bank at the stream's edge was the familiar miner's device—the rocker. In the center of the clearing, on the upturned roots of a tree stump, a few articles of clothing were hung to dry.

Even in the descending dusk, the deathly pallor of the man digging the trench was obvious. Sweat rolled down his leathery, weather-beaten face. And now he threw off his black felt hat—to wipe his forehead with the back of his hand—and exposed a shock of gray hair.

The leader of the group watching, a big, heavy-set man with a jet black beard, seemed to grow impatient.

"C'mon Farrell," he rasped. "It's deep enough—and we ain't got all day to waste."

Evans breathed softly and the shadows around his eyes darkened. Slowly, his lean hands reached down to his holsters.

. The gray-haired man called Farrell stopped shoveling earth and stepped out of the trench. He fronted the leader, pale but defiant,and shook his fist at him.

"Some day," he cried hoarsely, "yuh'll pay for this cold-blooded murder."

"Button yore lip," snapped the black-beard. "And get back there." He towered over the lean, wiry miner, gripped his arm, and—

"Not so fast, gents."

At the sound of the voice that drifted casually to them from across the clearing, the black-clad men whipped around like mongrels with tin-cans tied to their tails. They dove for hardware with practiced speed—then came up abruptly as they caught sight of a figure detach itself from a tree and move forward until he stood beneath the end of a low, leafy branch.

"Who are yuh?" cried the leader fiercely. "And what do yuh want here?" Two fox-eyes sat high up on his broad, pocked face. They tried to pierce the dusk to identify this intruder. The men behind him scowled darkly.

But the stranger's face was shadowed by hat and branch; and the features blurred. There was, however, no mistaking the identity and menace of the two black guns that jutted from his fists.

"I'm a right close friend of Mister Colt," drawled Evans. He wiggled the weapons suggestively. "Better tell yore *amigos* to remain hitched till I ask some questions—"

His right-hand gun bucked suddenly as he laid a shot down across the feet of a lank, scar-faced member of the black-clad band. The latter, on the far end of the shallow ditch, apparently thinking himself unobserved, had reached for his six-shooter. He changed his mind abruptly as the dirt showered his feet; and his hand froze to his side.

"I ain't foolin'," observed Evans calmly. A thin coil of blue-white smoke drifted lazily from the gaping black muzzle of his gun. He made a loose, idle shape standing there in the blur of the tree. But there was a grim threat of violence in the subtle undercurrent of his drawling voice, and the unexpectedness of his appearance.

Into the gray-haired miner's faded blue eyes leaped a sudden gleam of hope.

"Whoever yuh are mister," he cried desperately, "yuh got to help me. These hyenas—" He moved to step away from the trench.

"Stay put, Farrell!" roared the pock-faced man, still grasping the miner's arm in his huge, hairy paw. "And shut up! And yuh, mister, if yuh want to keep yore nose clean, stay out of someone else's business." His glance flared bellicosely at the armed man confronting him.

Bide Evans' skin tightened around his lips, and his gray eyes, flecked with queer lights, glinted oddly. Yet when he spoke, it was in the same deceptively mild voice.

"Yuh're a stubborn gent," he said evenly. "But I'm kind of patient myself. Matter of fact, I'm goin' to count all the way up to three. If yuh don't let go of Mr. Farrell's arm when I get up there—I'm goin' to put a bullet through

21

yore right knee cap. I saw a man once who couldn't use his leg for four years after that happened to him—"

With a baffled cry of rage, the leader released Farrell, thrust him forward and sent him sprawling on his face into the dirt.

A pulse high up in Evans' temple began to pound. But he relaxed as he watched the gray-haired man pick himself up. Then he put a question to him.

"What was that yuh were diggin' there, Farrell?"

"My grave!" cried the latter, hoarsely. "Them claim-jumpers rode into my camp ten minutes ago, stole my gold and told me to start shovelin' dirt—"

"Yuh lyin' son!" roared the heavy-set leader. "Yuh're the one who jumped this claim. It's registered in the name of a friend of mine." He gave vent to a short laugh, incomprehensible to the Texan.

"That ain't true," declared Farrell hoarsely, appealing to Evans. "Me and my pard been prospectin' Dutch Diggin's two weeks now—since the Gulch's sheriff got himself stretched. Yesterday we located this claim, and Ming Foy —that's my pard—went to register it at the Claims Office in Hangman's Gulch."

The fox-eyed man sneered and laughed sarcastically.

"Farrell's talkin' through his hat," he said, addressing Evans. "Don't know why I have to explain this to yuh. But this claim was worked three weeks ago. Then Matt had to go to Frisco, so he asked me to register it for him. Wal—I clean forgot to do it till yesterday. Then I decided to come out here to make sure everythin' was all right—when I run into this windbag, Farrell. The whole town knows he's a liar. Bet there ain't even no Ming Foy. Who ever heard of makin' a Chinaman a pardner? So the boys and me figgered on throwin' a little scare into him."

"It ain't so," cried Farrell, desperately, again to Evans. "Ming Foy's my pardner and as good as any white man. And I am a stranger in these parts. They don't know me in town—'cept Larson. He owns the general store. I don't even know how this *hombre* here learned my name. Never seen him before in my life." He hesitated a fraction as a thought semed to strike him. "By the great horn spoon, I do. Ming went to town to enter the claim. If someone else's name is on this piece of diggin', it's—it's because they stole the information from Ming and entered it themselves. That's why Ming didn't get back this mornin' like

22

he was supposed to. And they weren't foolin—" he pointed to the five men. "They were goin' to fill that grave with Ed Farrell's body."

"Yuh're *loco*," declared the leader. "The claims clerk wouldn't register the same claim twice—would he?" His manner suddenly became friendly. He fetched a small, leather bag from his pocket and tossed it to Farrell. "Tell yuh what, Farrell. That's the gold I took from yuh 'cause it rightfully belongs to my friend Matt. Wal—yuh go to town, and if yuh don't find Matt Evans' name down on the record—"

"Whose name?" A breath seemed to stir the leaves over the Texan's head—although no wind blew.

The big man squinted hard, trying again to make out the face of the man under the tree. But the dusk had deepened, and if it was difficult before, it became impossible now.

"Matt Evans—" he answered.

"Be back from Frisco tomorrer," put in the lank, scarfaced member of the band.

"Shut-up!" roared the leader, turning. Then with surprising agility, he suddenly leaped aside, shouting, "Gut-shoot him, Lem."

The man called Lem had spoken to get his leader's attention. While the latter had been talking, Lem had cautiously drawn his gun, being partially out of direct vision of the Texan. Now, he fired.

The redheaded Texan was a veteran of many gun battles, yet this once they almost caught him off guard. Still his movement was but a heart-tick behind the big man's. He lunged backward and sideward in the same motion and snapped a shot with either gun. He crashed to his knees, went down on an elbow—then leaped to his feet, leveled guns smoking.

"Freeze, *hombres!*" The command in his voice nailed their moving arms and shifting legs to the spot. All except the scarred, black-clad man named Lem.

He had fired once, and then two bullets blasted his chest. He cried out in brief torment, and the gun slipped from his twitching hands. His knees buckled, then he sagged suddenly in the middle, caved and pitched forward on his face into the ditch.

"Farrell," ordered the Texan. "Remove their hoglegs, then take the rifles out of their saddle boots."

23

The gray-haired miner did the job with alacrity, despite the glowering, hostile looks cast at him.

"I ain't never been crossed but once," cried the heavy, thick-set leader, grimly. "And that *hombre* wasn't happy long. I ain't seen yore face clear, mister, but I heard yore voice—and I'll be listenin' for it."

"Pick up yore amigo and get movin'," ordered the Texan. "That was a mighty interestin' story yuh told, *hombre*. Almost believed yuh. Better go before yuh tell another—maybe that this Matt Evans not only staked this here claim, but also is sheriff of Hangman's Gulch."

The gang's leader, astride his horse by now, looked incredulous a moment, then suddenly threw his head back and roared with laughter. His men joined in as they rode out of the clearing. The body of the dead man, hitched to the saddle of his horse, trailed after them.

For a short time nothing was heard but the receding sound of men laughing. Then it mingled with roil of the river, and faded. The Texan listened, eyes intent, puzzled. Then he shrugged his shoulders and holstered his guns.

"Do yuh know Matt Evans?" he asked Farrell.

"No," replied the gray-haired man. "Wait—'pears to me I heard the name in Hangman's Gulch. Matt Evans? He—he ain't a friend of yores, is he?" he asked hurriedly.

For a moment the Texan was silent, seemed to be turning something over in his mind. Finally he spoke.

"No," he said softly, almost to himself. "He ain't a friend of mine—he's my brother." The knuckles on his clenched fists were white. And a strange light blazed in his eyes.

"Found him," he murmured. "Found him."

4. Election Night

THE SUN had already set and darkness saddled the clearing. Yet distant peaks still shone faintly in memory of the just-faded sun. But the memory was brief and fast-vanishing in face of the avalanche-in-reverse of shadows that swifted up the slopes, to draw the black-purple mantle of night over them.

24

The wiry placer miner led the way into the lean-to. Bide Evans heard him fumble around in the dark. Then a match flared, and a candle stuck into the throat of a bottle sent its dull, yellow light probing into the shack's shadows. In another moment, a second bottle joined the first on the table with a lighted candle in its neck.

"If yuh're headin' for town," said Evans briefly, "we can ride in together."

"Sure," agreed Farrell. "Say, I don't know how to thank yuh. Hey pard—yuh're bleedin'."

The double-barreled candles threw light on a deepening red patch high up on the Texan's left arm.

"I reckon I be," murmured Evans. He had felt a slight stab of pain at the time of the shooting, but had forgotten it in the ensuing scene.

Ed Farrell grabbed up a bucket near the door. "I'll get some water from the stream." He turned. "Say, if yuh're Matt Evans' brother, yuh must be an Evans, too?"

"Good guess, Farrell," said the redheaded Texan, smiling faintly. "The handle's Bide Evans." He might have added: "Recently sheriff of Holman County, town of Dudley, Texas," but did not.

Evans took his shirt off. The wound, still bleeding slightly, he saw, was a two-inch gash across the fleshy part of his arm.

Then Ed Farrell came in, visibly excited, slogging water over the top of the bucket.

"I been a dumb fool," he cried. "That must've been Black Henry and the Hounds. I been warned against 'em."

"Hounds?" said Bide Evans. "Who are they?"

"Heard tell," replied Farrell, "they was chased out of Sacramento for killin's, startin' fires, and robbin' stores." He had torn a clean cloth into strips and was washing Evans' gash.

"And Black Henry?"

"He got the reputation," answered the oldster, fixing the bandage, "of bein' the slickest article this side of Truckee Pass." He frowned. "That's what worries me."

"What?" Evans asked, slipping into his shirt, and then vest.

"Maybe Black Henry," said Farrell slowly, "did enter a claim for yore brother?"

"Don't yuh fret, Farrell," Evans said. "If it was entered in Matt's name, I promise yuh'll get it back." A

25

thin smile cracked through the grim look his face held. "Is it worth gettin' back, Ed?"

In answer, the oldster brought out the little leather pouch Black Henry had thrown him and tossed onto the table. It struck solidly.

"Two days," he cried, excitement eating through his voice like acid. "And we ain't begun to take it out yet." He hesitated a moment. "If it weren't for yuh, Evans—I was thinkin' when I went down to the stream—that I'd like yuh to—become our pardner. Ming would sure say yes."

"Thanks, Ed," Evans said, shaking his head. "But I didn't come to California for gold. 'Sides, I expect to pull out of here in a couple of days."

The oldster's face fell. "If yuh should change yore mind," he said earnestly, "the offer remains open. Well, let's go. I'm gettin' worried about Ming."

A big, early moon split the night darkness and polished the earth's surface with frost-like silver. The two men followed the water-course westward, the oldster up behind Evans.

"Think we'll meet up with our 'friends' in town?" asked Evans.

" 'Tain't likely," replied Farrell. "Sam Larson told me there's a kind of war goin' on 'tween the Hounds and the Vigilante Committee—"

"Vigilantes? Ain't there no law in the Gulch?"

"Yuh mean a sheriff?" demanded the gray-haired man. "Not for the past two weeks. Last one was found hangin'; one before that, shot. By the great horn spoon!" He slapped his thigh. "I clean forgot. There's an election tonight—for a new sheriff."

Like a cold gust of wind, a premonition scraped the warmth from Bide Evans' lean face. The memory of laughing, black-clad men suddenly weighed heavily on him.

"Who's runnin'?" His voice rustled with the sharpness of stiff paper rubbed together.

"Don't recollect," answered Farrell. "Brother expectin' yuh?" he asked after a pause.

Evans half-twisted in saddle, stiffening.

"No," he said. But he knew that his tension had escaped through his voice, for Farrell said quickly:

"Sorry, Bide. Didn't mean to—"

"That's all right, Ed," Evans said. "It's a kind of surprise—family affair."

A bitter, ironic smile rolled unchecked across Bide Evans' face. If only it had been a family affair!

Perhaps it would have been better if he had never found Matt? Perhaps his pride of family was wrong? Then giving up his sheriff's badge because of what had happened was also wrong. But he knew it went beyond that. A man had to bear the responsibility for his deeds. A man had to give, and take back what he gave. And a man had to pay for what he got. Those were the lessons the hard, tough years had beaten into him. Lessons that showed up in his thin, half-smile, in the quickness of his eyes, in the faint scar whose track traced a small, wicked pattern across the side of his neck.

"There she be, Bide," suddenly cried Ed Farrell, a tinge of excitement riding his voice. "Hangman's Gulch."

"She's sure salty-lookin'," murmured Evans.

Loud noise and clamor rode the crowded main stem. Flares stuck into the earth on either side, and brilliantly lighted stores and buildings made the street a solid octaggonal block of yellow light.

"Plenty of rot-gut spilled tonight," cried Farrell, the town's mood hooking onto his voice. He flung his arm up. "Them must be the election banners, yonder. But can't make out what they say."

Toward the center of the town, Evans saw several white streamers strung overhead, across the street. But like Farrell, was unable to discern what was lettered on them. A cool down-draught from the surrounding hills kept tugging and pitching the banners.

They dismounted and the loose, swirling ends of the milling stream of men lapped out at them and sucked them in. Evans used his elbows and shoulders to wedge his way through. Farrell, behind, lifted his voice to make himself heard.

"If we get separated," he cried, "I'll meet yuh later at the Palace Saloon. I'm goin' to be lookin' for Ming."

Progress was slow and difficult, then Farrell tugged at his sleeve.

"Look!" yelled the oldster.

The redheaded Texan followed Farrell's pointing finger —then froze suddenly in his tracks. The warm light faded

27

from his eyes, and his shoulders hunched up, as if a chill had struck him.

" 'Matt Evans for Sheriff'!" cried Farrell, reading the bold black letters on the waving streamer overhead. "Hey, Bide! Yore brother's runnin' for sheriff! Ha! Ain't that a surprise?"

"Yeah, Ed," he said tonelessly. "It's sure a surprise."

" 'Vote for Tay Brown'," said Farrell, reading the second banner aloft. "Ha!" he laughed. "If Matt's anythin' like his brother Bide, Mr. Brown don't have no chance a-tall. No sir!"

A flat, hard grin worked its way off Bide Evans' face. "Hope not," he muttered.

"Huh?" demanded the blue-eyed oldster, not hearing him in the street din. "Heck!" he cried. "That means Black Henry did try to pull a whizzer on us with that story of his."

"I gave yuh my word, Ed," said Evans slowly, "that if yore claim had Matt's brand on it, I'd get it back for yuh." He turned abruptly and leading the black by the bridle plunged through the crowd.

A pent-up, restless feeling suddenly rode the redhead. His powerfully muscled body cried aloud for action— ached for the escape he found in its swift, violent flow.

He angled across the street toward the dark open doors of a stable.

"Putting up," he told the hostler. By the light off the street he took care of his horse. He felt the man's eyes on his back. He turned abruptly and saw them turn away.

When he quit the stable the hostler, a rotund, greasy man who wore a Yankee straw hat and striped pants that threatened to fall off, called his stable boy.

"Go tell Wurt he's back," he said. And the kid raced out.

Bide had left Farrell outside, but now found him gone. He shrugged, got into the jostling, thrusting crowd. He saw a general store, climbed the three steps and walked in. A large lamp hung over the counter—the only light in the room.

A girl entered from a side room and came behind the counter.

"Can I help you?" she asked, smiling. "You're lucky— we were just about to close."

His glance went across the room and touched her face.

28

"Reckon I am lucky," he said slowly, coming forward. "I need a box of cartridges——.45 Colt."

The light of the lamp showered Kate Larson's head with a kind of gossamer sheen. She had brown, wavy hair, but now it had golden glints in it. She was slim-waisted in her white taffeta dress with brown ribbons frilling it, and walked with an easy, assured stride.

Her eyes were probing under his hat shadow and a puzzled look came into her face; then he came into the light, and her eyes grew cold.

"They're not for sale to you—Matt Evans."

A ghost of a smile brushed against the Texan's lips, then it was gone. Since he had seen the election banner he knew this would happen. It was on the tip of his tongue to tell this girl he was Bide Evans. That Matt was his twin brother. That people had always confused the two of them. But that there were ways of telling them apart. His eyes, for example, were gray, Matt s green; he was slightly taller than Matt; he had a scar on his neck—another, just acquired, high up on his left arm.

There were other ways, but she wouldn't believe him —just yet. No one would. Moreover, he admitted to a deep curiosity about Matt's life since the latter had fled Texas. So he did not tell her he was Bide Evans.

"Why not, ma'm?" he asked softly.

"Because you're a drunkard, a coward, and a killer!" she flared angrily.

He frowned. He didn't understand her anger. "Them's harsh words, ma'm," he baited her. "I may take a few drops now and then—"

"Now and then!" she laughed. "I'm surprised you're standing steadily on your feet." Kate Larson had inherited her father's honesty and lashing, stinging tongue, and was unafraid to use it.

Bide Evans winced—for his brother; felt anger. But he had laid down a plan of action and he was going to follow it.

He shrugged. "Yuh're a woman," he pointed out. "Yuh can say things a man might hesitate sayin'."

"Then why did you slink away after you announced you were running for office?" she demanded.

"Business in Frisco," Bide Evans said.

"I don't believe you have any business," Kate cried.

He shrugged his shoulders again—and spoke the words

uppermost in his mind. "Yuh got me pegged wrong, ma'm," he said. " 'Sides I ain't never killed anyone—"

"You shot former Sheriff West," she cried.

He paled at the lips; shadows skirted his eyes. He took a chance: "Self-defense, ma'm," he protested. Then saw the answer in her face. Somehow, oddly, he felt better for it.

"That's what they said," she cried, her eyes unfriendly. "But I believe you're mean, vicious and unscrupulous— and capable of anything."

"That's a right pretty dress yuh're wearin', ma'm," he drawled. He had caught her off guard and she flushed up to her eyes. She was beautiful, he decided. He followed up: "How come yuh're so interested in me?"

"I'm not!" she cried. "At one time, when you first came here, I thought we could be friends. But you changed that thought very quickly." There was disgust and loathing in her voice.

The door through which the girl had entered, opened, and a big-boned, wide-mouthed man came out.

"Are yuh ready, Kate?" asked the latter. Then he saw Bide. His eyes flashed and the blood rose to his face.

Bide Evans at once divined what he had suspected: That the girl was Larson's daughter and that this was Sam Larson.

"So yuh did come back, Evans?" cried Larson. "I figgered yuh put a greater value on yore worthless hide."

"I put my own value on my hide," Bide drawled. Then he spoke the words he knew Matt would have spoken: "That's kind of reckless talk, Larson." He was committed to wring the last drop of information about Matt from these two.

"Maybe so, Evans," cried Larson stiffly, watching Bide's arms. "But a gent of yore caliber ain't material for a lawman. And will never get to be." There was a latent threat in his voice.

"Yuh can never tell," drawled Bide. He saw Larson's eyes and shook his head. "I didn't come for shootin' purposes, Larson."

"One thing I'd like to know," demanded Larson. "Where yuh got all the money to buy out Jim Wurt's Star for tonight and give away whiskey like it was water? Yuh never worked a day since yuh came here, Matt Evans—"

High up in Bide's face, his temple throbbed violently.

He knew only too well where Matt had gotten the money. Suddenly, he sickened of the game. His voice grew tight.

"Since yuh won't sell," he said briefly, "I'll say good night." He tipped his hat to Kate Larson, and went out.

Father and daughter stared after him.

"He won't be elected, will he, Dad?" Kate asked finally.

"Not a chance," exclaimed Sam Larson. But there was a worried look in his eye.

5. Wanted: Matt Evans

"SHE HIT YUH off plumb center, Matt," muttered Bide Evans thinly, coming out of the store. "Ran away from Dudley—but yuh couldn't run away from yoreself, brother."

He sighted a hotel diagonally up the street and set out for it, breasting the crowd. He brought up suddenly. then shook his head. "Nope—couldn't be the same party.

"Did Larson say, 'Jim Wurt'?" he cried. He frowned, He wouldn't be the owner of a saloon. The Wurt I knew never owned anythin' but a runnin' iron—" Again he shook his head.

The redheaded Texar made it across the thronged street. A thick, unsteady voi e reached for his ear. He turned and found a small, b ear-eyed, stubble-faced man mumbling at him. The little man's limbs were as unsteady as his voice.

"D'ja vote yet?" was the red-eye's query.

Bide reached out a hand in time to save the little man from falling. "Ain't votin' this election, pard," he said, smiling.

"Zat so?" cried the other, blinking, swaying dangerously. "But that ain't right, friend." He had thrown up his hand to point, but now used it to balance himself erect.

"Why not?" asked Bide, amused.

"The first dooty of a citizen is to vote." The little man got it out in one breath.

"Maybe yuh're right, pard," admitted Bide. "But I don't rightly know who's the best candidate."

Stubble-face nearly fell over himself in his eagerness to instruct.

31

"Matt Evans!" he cried. "That's yore candeedate. For the best sheriff in California. Yessir!" He raised his fist to bank it into his palm. He lost balance and fell.

Bide helped him to his feet. "What's this *hombre's* qualifications?"

"Qualeefications?" The little man was plain amazed. "He's got 'em. All candeedates have 'em. Wouldn't be candeedates if they didn't have 'em—would they? And there wouldn't be no 'lection without candeedates, would there? So yuh vote for Matt Evans."

Bide shook his head dubiously. "I don't know—"

"Now lissen to me, friend." Stubble-face took Bide into his confidence. "Yuh just mosey down to the Star, and tell 'em Charley Oaks sent yuh. That's me. You'll get all the red-eye yuh can hold—and I'll tell yuh somethin' else. The *hombre* who can vote the most times gets a hundred dollars." He became sad. "I voted only six times 'fore they threw me out. Maybe yuh can do better, friend." Then something else occurred to him and he caught Bide's arm. " 'Nother thing. They got a troupe of actors there. Won'erful impersonator. Hun'red wigs. Very good."

"I'll see, Mr. Oaks," said Bide. He watched the little man stagger into the crowd and vanish. "Maybe I'll drop by at the Star later," he mused.

He had almost made the hotel when once more he was intercepted. A black-frocked man darted out of the brown shadows of an alley, clamped a hand on Bide's arm and dragged him back into the shadows.

The man's carefully groomed hair had become disheveled and he was breathing heavily.

"Matt," he cried angrily. "I told yuh not to come back 'til tomorrer."

Bide Evans' eyes went over this man's face; then he suffered a shock of recognition. Sam Larson had said it right. And what he, Bide, thought couldn't be, could. In the rapid glance he bestowed on him, he saw that the man hadn't changed much. Just the mustache was new— and the store clothes. The pressure on his arm tightened. He shook the hand off.

"Damn it, Matt," cried the other. Once more he seized Bide's arm. This time Bide was not so gentle.

The well-dressed man gasped aloud and his forehead turned red. "Why yuh—" he began.

"I wouldn't do that, Wurt," drawled Bide. His elbows had gone back at an angle, tense, hooked. "The last time yuh tried, I had to throw yuh out of a saloon in Dudley. Remember?"

Jim Wurt stepped back as if he had received a blow. His face drained blood; his lower lip dropped. There was no doubt Wurt remembered.

"Bide Evans!" he gasped.

Bide nodded. "Sure surprised to see yuh here, Wurt," he said slowly. "Didn't know yuh and Matt were together."

Wurt pulled himself together, fast. The blood came back to his face; and his black eyes became expressionless. There was a hard core in Wurt, and it showed in the brief, curt smile he gave Bide.

"Matt and I ain't together," he said evenly. "We met here in the gulch by accident. He just asked for my advice—and I gave it to him; that's all."

"Kind of funny advice to give a gent runnin' for office," said Bide slowly. "To stay out of town 'til after election."

Wurt shrugged his shoulders. "Not my look-out," he declared. "Matt's a grown man and does what he wants. Anyhow, he's got a couple of friends lookin' after his vote-gettin'."

Bide said, "Sure looks like. And it was mighty nice of yuh, Wurt, to give over yore saloon to try and get Matt elected."

Wurt shook his head. "I'm a businessman, Evans," he said, frowning. "Matt rented the saloon for this one night. Anythin' wrong in that, Sheriff?"

"The question is on the word, 'sheriff'—ain't it, Wurt?" A faint smile flickered past Bide's thinned lips. "Guess it'll make yuh feel better when I tell yuh I left my badge in Dudley."

Wurt's face showed nothing; so with his voice. "Why should it make me feel better?"

"Because yuh were a cheap two-bit rustler, Wurt," said Bide softly.

"That's a danged lie!" cried Wurt angrily. "Yuh never had anythin' on me."

"Not," admitted Bide evenly, "until after yuh left—when we found yore irons. Got to admit yuh played the game pretty smart, Wurt. But by then we didn't care no

33

more; the people of Texas were glad to be rid of a gent like yuh."

"Don't know what yuh're talkin' about," cried Wurt. " 'Sides, nobody in this town would believe yuh. I been an honest saloon keeper for six months. They'd take my word against any saddle tramp's."

Bide Evans flushed, laughed briefly. "Yuh're sure dandied up, Wurt," he said. "Almost makes yuh look respectable—"

"I am respectable—and law abidin'!" snapped Wurt.

Bide Evans shrugged his shoulders. "Glad to hear it," he said. "But I didn't come lookin' for yuh. Let me ask yuh one question, Wurt."

"What's that?" demanded Wurt tonelessly.

"Yuh didn't quit Dudley," said Bide, "until a week or so after Matt lit out. Yuh know what happened. How come yuh let him run for sheriff's office here?"

Wurt picked his words carefully. "I don't hold no man's past against him," he said. "I been an underdog once myself—and I know how it feels. If a man wants to ride a straight trail, it ain't for Jim Wurt to throw stones at him, or pull him off his hoss. 'Sides, everybody felt the old man got what was comin' to him—the old skinflint."

"That don't make any difference," said Evans sharply. Yet, he reflected, there was a measure of truth in what this man said. "I'm takin' Matt back to Texas with me."

Wurt shrugged his tailored shoulders. "Too bad," he said. "Just when Matt's about to make a new beginnin'. Maybe if it wasn't for the Evans family pride, yuh wouldn't be so hot after yore own brother."

It was a shrewd thrust. Everyone in Southwest Texas knew the Evanses had been the first to pioneer there; that the tremendous Circle E spread was the biggest in the section; that Luke Evans was a stiff, unbending man and father.

Evans observed Wurt through narrowing eyes. There was a smartness in this man he hadn't suspected. It was a mistake, he saw, to underrate any man.

He said, "Be kind of awkward if Matt should win the election."

"For yuh." The words slipped out before Wurt could check them. He bit his lips.

Evans saw the humor, smiled grimly. "Well—it won't

matter." Then, "But yuh don't figger he'll be elected do yuh, Wurt?"

The light in Wurt's black eyes was oblique. "Don't know," he said.

The lean Texan smiled again, this time thinly. "Understand Matt's due back tomorrer. If he shows up tonight—it'd be better if he didn't know I was here. *Sabe?*"

"I won't tell him," said Wurt. He walked away.

The hotel's narrow lobby was gloomy, with a raw dirtied desk and a stairway going up beyond it. He lifted the pen at the desk and scratched, "Bide Evans," into the soiled register. A man came from the dining room and went behind the desk. He did not look at the register, but said, "Yuh're back."

Evans' glance ran over him coldly, killed the smile that was forming. "Send up a hot tub of water, *pronto*," he said. "What room?"

"Take Number Six," said the other, twitching.

The stairway creaked as he took his weight up to the landing. He blinked uncertainly in the dim-lighted corridor, then found his room.

He got out of his vest and shirt—and waiting for the tub, began to shave. It was hard, painful going, scraping away the accumulated growth. In the meantime, his mind lay back on his meeting with Jim Wurt. It was little short of coincidence that when he finally came up with Matt, he should find Wurt there.

Back in Texas, Jim Wurt had taken up a piece of Government land next to the Circle E. He rarely came to town and he had no friends. Where he had come from had been a mystery; and how he was building up his herd, another. A few missing cows made little difference in a land where most ranchers started their herds that way. But Bide, as sheriff, had not chosen to take this view, and when Matt began to be seen drinking in his company, intensified his search for proof. But somehow, Wurt's activities managed to escape detection. Nevertheless, a blow-up finally came and he had thrown Wurt out of the town saloon.

Then, shortly after Wurt had sold out and quit Dudley, he had found proof of the latter's cattle-running activities. But then it was too late. And now, he thought, he would let by-gones be by-gones.

35

"But it's kind of hard to believe," he muttered, dousing his face with water and then rubbing it dry. When he had done, he gazed momentarily at himself in the cracked mirror. An impulse prompted him to fetch a folded paper from his shirt. He spread it flat underneath the mirror and looked from it back to the mirror again. A faint enigmatic smile played over his face.

It might have been his face that looked from the Wanted Poster—the features were identical—but it wasn't. For it had Matt Evans' name beneath the picture. And above it the legend: WANTED FOR MURDER—$1000 REWARD—DEAD OR ALIVE.

Underneath the name was the information that Matt Evans had broken into the Bank of Dudley, shot and killed the owner of the bank, Abe Symes, and had robbed the safe of ten thousand dollars.

A slight scraping sound brought Bide Evans around fast. Whipping to the door, he pulled it open, himself swinging back behind it. Long, hard years riding danger's trail had bred in him a caution about opening doors.

But there was nothing here. He listened a fraction and then sidled out into the corridor, gun palmed. It was empty to his sweeping gaze. Frowning, he stepped back across the threshold, then stooped to pick up a piece of paper that had been left there.

He kicked the door shut and strode to the uncurtained window. He had a view of the entrance. No one came out.

Under the lamp light at the dresser, he unfolded the single crease and read the words written roughly on it. It was a brief note:

"Get out of town, *pronto,* Evans—if you aim to stay healthy."

A smile made thin wrinkles around the corners of his gray eyes. "Not a very hospitable town," he murmured. "Just came and they want me to leave." He shook his head and his smile grew wider. "But which Evans do they mean?" he mused. "Matt or me?" He sat down on the edge of the bed and considered the matter.

There was only one person in the Gulch who knew him as Bide Evans—and that was Jim Wurt; aside from Ed Farrell, whom he ruled out for obvious reasons. There was a good reason for Wurt to have sent the note. The one-time rustler might have been afraid that his past would

36

be revealed and so injure his present standing in the Gulch. Moreover, Wurt hated him—as much as he despised Wurt.

Then, there was the other alternative. Several people believed they were seeing Matt, when they were looking at him. He suddenly remembered the look in the straw-hatted hostler's eye, and identified it as recognition. Then there was Sam Larson and his daughter, Kate.

For a brief moment, his reasoning went off on a tangent. Then there was the hotel owner. And any number of people he had passed on the street. If Larson—and even Wurt had supposed him to be Matt, so would anyone else.

If that were the case, and he now believed it to be so, then the note was addressed to Matt. He nodded, remembering Larson's words.

"Looks like Matt ain't so popular in the Gulch," he mused. Then he smiled ruefully, realizing that although the note was intended for Matt, it didn't lessen the danger to himself.

A knock sounded against the door. Two men carried in a steaming tin tub of water and set it down on the floor. He flipped them some coins, and they went out.

Refreshed, Bide Evans climbed into his clothes and blew out the lamp. With his hand on the doorknob, he changed his mind, and went across the room to the window. As he looked down into the Gulch's well-lighted main stem, his lips pulled into a thin, tough smile.

The street flowed with men, and anything stationary stuck out like a sore thumb. Across the street, a man lolled against the corner of a store. The latter's eyes had been directed up, at the window. Now he was motioning to another man stationed a hundred feet away against a stable door. And there was a third man posted at the far corner of the hotel, his thumbs idling in his gunbelt. They made, Evans noted, a kind of rough triangle. He nodded slowly.

Here was a game with which he was familiar. A game whose rules and meaning had cost him much to learn. The first play had been the note. Soon, the next would be made. But he would be ready for it. Ready, despite the fact that it was really Matt's game.

Irony creased his face. No matter what he might tell

37

them, they would disbelieve him. Whether he liked it or not, he had to be Matt Evans until the play was over.

For a moment, he stood there, shadows forming deep pools around his eyes. Then he went out of the door, down the stairs and into the dining room.

6. Brothers Meet

THE ROOM was rectangular, with tables and a lunch counter. A few dusty lamps hung from the low ceiling; and a door in the center led to the street. There were two men in the room, eating at the far corner table. Evans chose a table at the shoulder of the counter and sat facing the door. At his left was the blank partition of the hotel.

A Mexican waitress came out of the kitchen. He ordered and told the girl, *"Muy pronto."* He had an idea that when he didn't appear at the hotel door, they were going to come looking for him.

In a while they drifted in, singly, through the street entrance. Lean, beady-eyed men, with hardened lines in their faces, and sagging gun belts. Too casually they seated themselves: one, at the corner table directly opposite Evans; the second, in the center of the room, at a tangent; and the third, at the middle of the counter.

It grew close and hot in the room, and Evans felt a quickening pulse beat in his neck. The rumble of mining talk made by the two men in the far corner sifted through the eating place with aimless intent. But the silence of the three newcomers grew heavy with the voice of trouble.

The man opposite, taller than the others, lighted a cigarette. It was a signal for the man at the counter to start talking.

"Came to ask yuh a question, Evans," the man said.

"What's the question?" he asked, his glance reaching out to the three of them.

"Yuh saw the note?"

"Question for question, friend," he said.

38

The man at the counter shook his head. "No," he said. "Did yuh see it?"

"Yeah."

"What's yore answer?"

He showed them a grim, tough smile, and drawled, "I ain't decided yet. Maybe I'll stay—maybe I'll get."

"Listen, Evans." The one at the counter raised his voice. "Nobody wants yuh here. Yuh're gettin' a chance to leave in one piece. Why don't yuh take it?"

Something in here got tight and heavy. Something that pressed down on Evans' head. Then he realized it was the silence, tightening around him like a vise, ringing him— cutting him off.

The three men watched him through half-slit eyes, watched him with cold, pitiless intent, watched him ceaselessly.

He said, "How much time yuh gents givin' me to decide?"

The one at the counter barked, "No time." His voice went high-pitched, ricocheted off the low ceiling and jumbled to a vague murmur.

The silence stretched thin; strained to the breaking point. Evans' attention lay steady on these three; on the angle at the crook of their elbows; on the taut pressure of their shoulders against the back of the chairs; on the bright surface glint in their eyes.

This was the play, he knew. There was no turning back. Idly, he wondered what Matt would have done. Then, as always, he got tired of the game—and threw in his chips.

"Then I reckon I'll stay," he said.

"No yuh don't," yelled the counter one, pounding the pine boards sharply, to snare his attention.

But his eyes were riveted on the other two, now. The tall man was shoving back from the table to get his guns in the clear; and the other's arms were riding down fast. In a sightless blur of speed Bide Evans slapped his holsters and simultaneously tipped back in his chair.

The dining room split wide open with the crash and roar of six guns; and in the acrid odor of burnt gunpowder swirled through the room in blue-white streamers.

As he went over backward, the Texan set up a murderous crossfire, laying his left hand gun under his right and letting it run red at the man at the center table; in

39

the meantime holding his bucking, right hand gun on a straight bead with the tall one.

Then he crashed to the floor and rolled over to the protective shoulder of the counter. He had hooked his boot into a leg of the table and pulled it down as he fell.

The table banged down in front of him, giving him a sort of angled cover. But there was only one gun blasting away now, in a raking fusillade along the top of the counter. Being at its bottom, gave Evans a moment's respite. Enough to see the effect of his shots.

The tall man's guns were but half clear of leather, when hot lead spattered his chest with two splotchy, red rings. He was moving back at the time, and his impetus carried him sliding off the chair. He pitched sideward and rolled over on his face—to lie motionless.

The center table one never knew what hit him. His descending hands had barely touched Colt butts, when molten death sang him a fast tune. A bullet drilled a neat hole in his head and he slumped over the table. He lay like a man who had fallen into a drunken sleep.

The firing suddenly ceased. The rumbling echo of gun talk wandered remotely around the room. Evans lay pressed against the shadowed end of the counter and waited. Time grew rigid, receded, washed back again. The sudden clatter of boots beating across the floor broke the silence. Then the door slammed.

Slowly, Evans picked himself up, restored his guns and brushed himself off. The men in the corner were still there, motionless, staring.

Evans righted his table, put two coins down and walked through the arched doorway into the lobby. Over his shoulder he saw the Mexican waitress come cautiously out of the kitchen, stare at the two dead men, then yell back that she was going for the undertaker. The twitch-mouthed man watched him with graying eyes, but Evans said nothing to him and went out the hotel entrance.

Out in the street, the sign of the Palace Saloon caught his eye and he remembered his promise to meet Ed Farrell there. He moved with the throng. The night was yet young, he saw, the crowd still fresh.

Gun-fare somehow left a bad taste in his mouth. It had always been that way. Even the years he had spent as sheriff of Dudley. And although he regretted the cause, he had been glad of the opportunity to lay his badge away. He was eager to take over the job of ramrodding the Circle E. A job that rightfully should have been shared between himself and Matt. But it had been apparent from the very beginning that the red headed Evans twins were to share nothing but trouble.

Whatever the reason, Matt had early turned into a wild youth, bitter, defiant. Never on the spread, he had taken to drinking and running with a tough crowd.

His wife being an ailing woman, Luke Evans, and Bide as well, concealed as much as they could from her. To his dubious credit, Matt didn't care. It even galled him that Bide covered up for him.

"Mind yore own business," he often yelled at Bide.

"Why don't yuh shake out of it, Matt?" Bide had asked.

"Yuh make me sick," Matt had cried, his face showing disgust.

When Bide became sheriff, Matt drifted away. Ugly rumors came back to the Circle E. Then, two years ago, Matt turned up, wilder than ever. There had been a wild scene and Luke Evans threw Matt out. In bitter contempt, Matt hung around Dudley, baiting Bide, brewing gall at the Circle E.

Then a miracle had occurred—or almost a miracle. Matt Evans married the daughter of the town banker, Abe Symes, and turned into a devoted husband.

But bad blood had developed immediately between Matt and his father-in-law, and the latter publicly cursed Matt.

For one year things had gone smoothly. Then one day Matt came back leading a horse, his face a black mask. The body of his wife, dead, lay over the saddle. The horse had stumbled and she had been thrown . . .

Matt took to steady, hard drinking; and was seen frequently in Jim Wurt's company. Then came the final blow.

One morning, early, returning to Dudley from an overnight trip, he found a crowd gathered outside the bank.

"Symes dead—shot," they told him as he reined up. "Safe cleaned out."

When he went in, he found Symes on the floor, a gold coin-charm belonging to Matt in his right hand. There was a heavy bruise on the back of Symes' head; and the doors of the safe were wide open.

Symes had been heard arguing the night before with

Matt, blaming the latter for his daughter's death. Words almost led to blows. Then later, Matt was seen leaving the bank.

There were a couple of things that had troubled Bide at the time. The charm had been found in Symes right hand; but Symes' right arm was paralyzed. He never could use it; and tried to hide that fact from the world. That, and the hoof prints he had found underneath the bank's back window that morning. They were obviously several hours old and led him to think there might have been another man along with Matt. Yet only Matt had been seen leaving the bank.

And when Matt was found to have skipped the country, his guilt was confirmed.

The blow struck Bide's mother down and she never left her bed. But his father cried out for vengeance—for justice—even against his own flesh and blood. And Bide, sharing the family pride, took off his badge and set out on the trail.

Haze and sound and a flashing back-bar mirror filled the Palace saloon. Men stood three deep against the long bar, and crowded the poker and faro tables. A banner hung above the bar, "Tay Brown for Sheriff," it read.

Standing at the door, Evans' gaze went out, searching the room for Ed Farrell. But Farrell was not in the place. Then Evans' gray eyes held fast.

At one end of the saloon, where the Chinese band scraped, there was a kind of balcony, with some men and a girl around a table. The girl was Kate Larson. One of the men was her father; there were three or four others.

It was evident they were holding a party. A big champagne bottle was being tilted around; then the glasses lifted to a dark-faced, dark-clad man—whom Evans placed as a gambler.

Someone at the bar caught the scene and shouted raucously, "Three cheers for Tay Brown—the Gulch's next sheriff!"

The dark-faced man on the balcony smiled briefly and lifted his glass. A deafening roar reverberated through the saloon.

"Mr. Brown and his friends," muttered Evans, "wouldn't be so all-fired sure if they met Charley Oaks." He shrugged his shoulders. "But it won't make any difference."

Pulling his wide-brim well over his eyes, Evans drifted to the bar. In Dudley, his sheriff's badge told people he was Bide Evans. But Sam Larson yonder thought he was Matt. So would the rest.

He used his shoulders to wedge in and snagged a bottle and glass. He laid the price down on the mahogany and moved back against the wall. Then he saw Brown rise and rap the wooden balcony rail with an empty bottle.

"Friends," the latter said, when things quieted, "while we're waitin' for the election results, Miss Larson is goin' to favor us with a song." The crowd roared.

A man climbed into the chair at the piano, beneath the balcony and Kate Larson began to sing. She had a clear, sweet voice that brought fast silence to the large room.

With sudden abruptness, Kate Larson cut her song— to stare wide-eyed at someone in the center of the saloon.

Cold premonition clawing his spine, Bide swung his gaze around—and gasped softly.

A tall, lean-faced man stood alone on the cleared dance floor. He had doffed his sombrero, and the lamp above his head caught the red flare of his hair, and the green glint from his eyes.

"I will not sing," cried Kate Larson, "while Matt Evans is in the room."

A gasp sawed through the saloon like wind on autumn leaves.

"Yuh sure sing pretty, ma'm," said Matt Evans. "Didn't mean to interrupt yuh."

A thin smile skirted Bide Evans' lips. There was a kind of unpremeditated poise about his brother that he reluctantly admired.

"I don't think," Kate Larson said slowly, "you're welcome here, Mr. Evans."

Matt Evans swung his head in a half-circle. "Saloons are public places, Miss Larson," he said, his voice ruffled. "Any man can come in to buy a drink." He moved to the bar and stood with his back against it, facing the room.

He had been drinking, Bide saw, and his face was flushed and his eyes lighted. But Matt held his liquor on steady feet—and his voice was even.

Tay Brown was up beside the girl now, the scar along his jaw, red.

"Yuh heard Miss Larson, Evans," Brown cried. "She said what everybody feels."

"Why howdy, Mr. Brown," drawled the green-eyed redhead. "How's the vote-gettin' business?" A thread of insolence wound through his voice.

"Yuh're a bad one, Matt Evans," cried Brown fiercely, "and like to stir up trouble."

Bide watched the provoking grin spread over his brother's face.

"It ain't me that started the trouble," drawled the latter. "Why don't yuh ask Judge Carter where the blame falls."

The silver-goateed, black-frocked man who had been sitting beside Tay Brown, spoke up.

"He's right, gentlemen," he said reluctantly, stiffly. "Matt Evans isn't at fault."

"Thanks, Judge," said Matt, the grin covering his face completely. "Yore decision is accepted and approved."

Someone guffawed, but the sound choked off quickly into the deep silence.

Bide Evans pushed back slowly from his table. If he read the signs aright, Matt was building up a fire which was going to explode in his face.

But Judge Carter hadn't finished. "However right Mr. Evans may be," he said with a twinkle in his eyes, "it is my opinion that he would be wise to leave."

A large laugh ran around the room and stuck in the man-clusters at the tables.

Matt Evans made a lean, tough shape backed against the bar, his elbows hooked negligently onto it.

"Sorry I got to dissent from the judge's learned opinion," he said evenly, with only a faint trace of a smile left now. "But I just got back to town, and heard a party was bein' thrown for the next sheriff—" his speech slowed "—so I came."

"Yuh can't win the election," cried shaggy-headed Sam Larson, on his feet.

"Why not?" snapped Matt. His face was sharp.

"Because no honest folk would vote for yuh!"

Bide Evans watched the wild streak in his brother work its way through to the surface of his face.

"Then let the honest folk go to the Vigilantes for their

44

law—but if I'm elected, I'll wipe the Committee out," roared Matt Evans.

"Men," yelled Sam Larson, "are we goin' to let this hoodlum and his pack of wolves run the Gulch?"

Matt plucked his guns from leather with incredible speed and leveled them at the crowd.

"Maybe this'll help," he cried, grinning wolfishly.

Down at the edge of the bar, Bide caught a sudden gleam. His right hand went down in a blur of motion. The slap of his holster and the report of his Colt sounded almost simultaneously.

A howl went up at the bar as a man grasped a suddenly bleeding hand from which a gun had just been smashed.

Wheeling swiftly, Matt Evans saw the gun clatter to the floor, then turning back, watched the lean man who had fired restore his smoking Colt to leather and come slowly across the room.

Recognition flamed in Matt's green eyes. His nostrils flared and his lips went back wickedly, unsmiling.

"That was a favor, brother," he said harshly. "I didn't ask for it, but it was a favor. I'll pay it back."

7. Vigilantes

FOR SOME TIME after, there was speculation in the Gulch about the meeting and then the bloody fight between the two men who resembled each other so much that few could tell them apart. Speculation because the talk was carried on so low that no one heard what they said—except a few scattered, sharp-spoken words.

"Howdy, Matt," said Bide Evans.

"Howdy, Sheriff," said Matt, mockingly, guns still out.

Bide, shaking his head, heard the gust of surprise sweep the room.

"No more," he said evenly. "Not for six months. Gave it up a week after yuh hightailed it out of Texas."

Matt threw a quick, slanting glance around the room.

45

"Family pride—huh?" he jeered. "Brush-jumper tramples family name—huh?"

"Ma died when she heard," said Bide, shadows pulling around his eyes.

"Oh." Momentarily Matt's face lost its hard, bright indifference. "Sorry."

For a second, Bide felt a stab of sympathy for this stranger who was his brother. Then he remembered. He put the words out slowly:

"I promised dad I'd bring yuh back."

"What for?" Matt considered him warily.

"For killin' Abe Symes—" began Bide.

"Accident," said Matt, his face cold, his lips bitter. "He called me names no man could take. He hit me. I pushed him away—maybe too hard. But those names riled. He fell on his head." He lifted his shoulders, and let them fall.

"Then he was dead?" Bide asked softly, eyes narrowed.

"Yeah," said Matt. "Felt his pulse." He stood unmoved, his eyes cheerless. "The old buzzard had it comin' to him."

"A killin's a killin', brother," said Bide. "Anyone see it happen?"

The Gulch's candidate for sheriff shook his head. "No," he said.

"How come yuh didn't stay and tell about it, Matt?" demanded Bide, his voice low and patient. " 'Stead of movin' out?"

Matt showed him a contemptuous smile. "Who'd believe it when Matt Evans told it?" His smile ran out. "Folks saw me drinkin' that night; heard Symes and me argue. They'd swear I'd done it. 'Sides, I was tired of Dudley and planned to leave the next day anyhow. Didn't see no reason to change my plans."

"That all?" asked Bide.

"That's all," said Matt, his face showing nothing, hiding nothing.

Bide let his eyes wander around a tense, expectant room before he brought them back to Matt.

"I heard tell of another story," he murmured.

"Ain't interested," said Matt Evans.

"Yuh ought to be," advised Bide softly. "This one is about Symes with two .45 bullet holes in his head—and his safe picked clean."

Matt's eyes widened and the shadow of surprise lay in

them. Then his lips curled and he gave Bide a gray, derisive grin.

"Never heard of that story," he said.

Bide said, "Maybe this'll refresh yore memory." He fetched the Wanted poster from his pocket and gave it to Matt. Through lids that had crept close together, he watched his brother. There was something in this that didn't belong. Something that was out of shape.

A red tide poured into Matt's cheeks; and his eyes grew bright and glassy with the shine of solid anger.

"This thing is a lie!" Matt breathed. "A damn lie!" The Wanted poster became a small, creased ball of paper in his clenched fist.

Bide took an object from his pocket. "Recognize this?" he asked. It was a gold coin with a piece of chain linked through it.

Matt took it, holstering a gun. "Sure," he replied. "It's mine. Where'd yuh find it?"

"In Symes' right hand," murmured Bide.

Matt made a gesture of impatience. "The whole thing's crazy," he said. "I lost this 'bout a week before Symes died. I don't know anything about two bullet holes and ten thousand dollars."

A momentary flicker of doubt passed through Bide Evans' mind. Annoyed, he brushed it aside.

"That's why," he said, his lips twisting in irony, "folks say yuh're always broke. And that's why it was kind of hard for yuh to rent the Star Saloon tonight and give away enough free whiskey to flood the Gulch."

"For an *hombre* 'thout a star on his vest," gritted Matt, "yuh ask too damn many questions. I warn yuh, Bide—"

The gray-eyed Texan knew he had struck home. The telltale wild strain flushed Matt's face.

"Maybe *yuh* ought to warn yore friend Black Henry," said Bide, "not to file other folks' claims in yore name. Or maybe yuh don't know anything about that, either?"

There was a sudden blank look in Matt's eye. "That's right," he said.

Bide considered his brother a moment, then said briefly, "Yuh're lyin', Matt."

Matt fixed him with a controlled stare, gray and contained.

"Never cared much for that face of yore's, brother Bide," drawled Matt. "Expect I'll have to change it."

The scar on Bide's neck glowed red, and his lips flattened. "I came to take yuh back to Texas, Matt," he murmured, "And I'm goin' to."

"If yuh want me, brother," Matt taunted, holstering his other gun, "yuh'll have to come and get me."

Bide Evans swayed gently forward on the balls of his feet. "All right, Matt," he said. "Here I come."

Matt brought his arms up fast, but still not quite fast enough. Bide was moving even as he spoke. He gentled his brother with a solid clout on the jaw the rocked Matt back on his heels. Then moving in fast, he let fly with his left fist. Balled into an iron club, and with the heft of his shoulder behind it, his fist landed cleanly again on Matt's jaw. The blow's echo smacked through the room, like the whack of a beaver's tail on water, and Matt went slamming down into sawdust.

He bounded immediately to his feet, and grinning wolfishly, charged in. Matt fought with skill and cunning, and crashed through Bide's guard repeatedly.

Bide gave ground slowly, absorbing punishment—and giving it back. The thin smile that played around his lips tightened, grew grim. Here he was, at the end of the trail. He should have felt glad. But somehow, something had gone wrong—

His boot heel suddenly caught in a brass spittoon at the end of the bar and he went over on his back.

"Yuh drink too much," mocked Matt, waiting for him to come up.

Bide showed him a mirthless grin and leaped to his feet. Whatever other faults Matt may have had, Bide had to confess his brother fought cleanly.

Toe to toe the brothers swayed, pounding, hacking, beating at each other, the sound of their blows smacking like pistol shots.

Bruises sprang purple to their faces and blood flowed in a stream from Matt's nose. Oblivious now to the wide-eyed crowd, they fought on.

A red haze was forming over Bide's eyes; pain began to rack him, and he was panting hard. But he saw that Matt was worse off. One of the latter's eyes was half-closed and he was gulping air through his mouth, like a fish out of water. Long drinking bouts were taking their toll on Matt Evans.

A new sound abruptly impinged on Bide's senses: that

of a shouting crowd. And out of the corner of his eye, he saw that the saloon had gone taut and intent. Suddenly, his ear made sense out of the growing shout. Matt caught it too, for the latter's lips were going back in a slow, wide grin.

Matt let his hands slide down and hook on by the thumbs into his gun belt. He spoke gratingly, mockingly to his twin.

"I'm goin' to throw yuh in the jug, brother Bide," he said, "for resistin' an officer of the law."

By now the cry of the shouting crowd in the street rang solidly through the Palace Saloon's walls:—

"Matt Evans! Matt Evans!" they cried.

The situation had abruptly become awkward. His mind dizzy with the sudden need for immediate action, Bide came to a quick decision. With the speed of an angry polecat, he brought up his fist in a driving, wicked arc that landed with a pulpy echo on the point of Matt's jaw. "Sorry I had to do it," he muttered, as his brother toppled to the floor.

In a twinkling, he plucked his Colts from leather— But things had already begun to happen. As Matt started crumpling to the floor, Bide caught a fast glimpse of his miner friend, Ed Farrell, come in through the batwings with a Chinaman at his side.

Then the crackle of gunfire suddenly swept the saloon, and black-masked men came leaping in through the windows, shooting at the lights. A cry broke from the crowd.

"Vigilantes!"

Ten or twelve of them, they circled the room, and the lamps blinked out one by one. There was something ominous in their deliberate shooting. Then, with one light-bracket remaining, Bide saw they were converging on him. Or was it Matt, whose inert figure lay on the floor at his feet?

A hot flame suddenly burned in the Texan's mouth. His lips dried. Slowly, his guns leveled, he backed to the bar. Once more a six-shooter raked the increasing gloom. The last light slapped out. He felt rather than saw a blurry figure loom up behind him on the bar.

Shadows gave way to complete, ebony darkness as he whirled and triggered a shot at the leaping man. A cry of pain sawed through the room. Then clutching, muscular

49

hands laid hold of him and pinioned his limbs. Before he could resist, his Colts were torn from his hands.

With a desperate, angry upsurge, he cast off his captors and lashed out at them. He felt his fist sink deeply into a man's belly, heard the grunt. Again he threw his fist into the more solid darkness. Once more he connected.

Then they swarmed over him. Sobbing for breath, working his arms like pistons, Bide gave ground. Abruptly, it was all over. Noisy blackness crashed down on his head with a terrific jolt. The saloon floor tilted up in his face with explosive light. When it reached his shoulder, he wearily leaned on it and the brightness slowly faded.

He came to with a splitting head; gingerly he touched it. There was a hard lump in back, and he winced as his fingers found it.

He rolled over slowly and elbowed up. Gradually, as his eyes groped through the darkness, he saw that he was prisoner in a small, bare room.

He climbed cautiously to his feet, his knees threatening to buckle. He sought the near wall and put his shoulder against it. His face felt hot and sore from Matt's fist and the ache in his own right hand was pretty bad.

Then he became aware of the dull, reflected glow coming from a high barred window, and the windless echo of the town's noise that sifted in with it. He realized that he couldn't have been here very long; that the town was still celebrating election night.

"Them Vigilantes didn't come for *Bide* Evans," he muttered. "This whole business is gettin' monotonous."

Then the double irony in the situation loosened his lip-lines. "But he got to be sheriff, anyhow," he mused. "And that's goin' to make it kind of tough for me."

Six months he had trailed his brother, and now that he had found him—He shrugged his shoulders. There would be a way. He had always found it.

But first, he had to get out of here—to persuade the Vigilantes it was a case of mistaken identity. Then he would be free to deal with Matt. There were a few more questions he wanted to ask his brother.

Matt's story was impossible to believe. Yet—it had sounded unrehearsed; and Matt had *seemed* genuinely surprised on seeing the Wanted poster. Of course, Matt had been drinking that night. Moreover, it would be natu-

50

ral to deny the shooting; for outside of that, the death of Symes could have been accidental.

And then there was the charm, which Matt claimed he had lost a week before Symes' death. Equally disturbing was that it had been found in Symes' paralyzed right hand —not his good left.

Matt had claimed to be alone that night. That would rule out anyone else's share in the killing. Yet—if Matt's story *were* true—

He shook his head. His brother was apparently affluent. And the source of his funds, Bide was willing to wager, was the Dudley bank. Despite the fact that Matt had been in the gold fields for six months, Bide was certain his brother would sooner become respectful of the law than swing a pickaxe and pan a gravel bar.

A key scraped in the door latch. Yellow light sprang into the room in an oblong shaft. Then two armed men stood in the doorway, throwing grim shadows into the room.

"Come on out, Evans," one said curtly.

Bide Evans left the wall, and went into the next room.

There were about ten gun-belted men there, all wearing black masks up to the eyes. But it was something else that held him. The room shaped like a court. There was a judge's desk on a raised platform—the witness chair next to it. And on the chair's left, was another half-dozen, with men filling them: the jury. Only an audience was missing.

The "judge" was speaking now: "—so it's me or Number Eight," he was saying. "If he comes, I don't." Then his gaze snapped to the "prisoner." "Bring him before the bar," he ordered.

The Texan felt the prod of cold steel against his spine, and moved up until he stood facing the "judge." The latter's voice sounded familiar, and then Bide knew to whom it belonged: Sam Larson. He felt the latter's eyes scrutinizing him carefully.

"Yuh're in the Vigilante Court, Matt Evans," the "judge" said. "Turn around and let the jury have a look at yuh. Some of the boys figger maybe a mistake was made. I don't."

Bide turned to the jury and felt their eyes go over his face.

51

"Maybe if yuh asked me, gents," he said, "I'd be able to set yuh straight."

There was little hesitation on the part of the "jury."

"It's Matt Evans," they said, almost as one man.

Anger rose in Bide like a welling tide.

"I'm Bide Evans!" he snapped. "Matt's my brother. How many of yuh have seen me before to say, 'Yuh ain't Bide, yuh're Matt'?" His eyes swept them, cold gray. "None of yuh," he answered. "And even if yuh had, it'd be hard for yuh to tell, 'cause Matt and I are twins."

"Yuh been identified proper, Matt Evans," cried the "judge," nettled. "And the court is satisfied."

"But *I* ain't satisfied—" began Bide.

"Yuh was always good at makin' speeches," interrupted the "judge," "but it ain't goin' to do yuh any good this time. There ain't no law and order in the Gulch and yuh're one of the reasons. Yuh were elected sheriff tonight —God knows how—but yuh ain't never goin' to wear the badge. The law-fearin' folk of this town want a lawman they can trust. Number Four, bring in the first witness against the defendant."

8. The Trial

NUMBER FOUR Vigilante went to the door at the other end of the room and poked his head out. A man entered, blinked owlishly in the light.

"Set up here, Rivers," the "judge" told the latter.

Dan Rivers, the Gulch's printer and publisher of the weekly *Herald*, shifted his bulk slowly across the room and edged into the seat.

"Howdy, Matt," he said. His smile was neither friendly nor unfriendly.

An up-curve faintly wreathed Bide's lips. Although he had heard plenty about Matt, it seemed he was going to learn more—whether he liked it or not. He gave a brief, fatalistic shrug.

"Look, 'Judge' Larson," he said. "If I got to listen to yore case against Matt—I'd like a seat."

The "judge" hesitated a moment, then ripped off the black kerchief. It was Sam Larson.

"I ain't afeared of what yuh or yore hoodlums can do, Evans," he cried heatedly. "And I don't have to hide behind a mask." He turned to the "jury." "Yuh keep yore's on. No tellin'—"

"So he claims he ain't Matt," said Rivers. "That's mighty interestin'."

"We ain't got all night," cried Larson, irritated. "Tell the jury yore story, Dan."

"Well," replied the printer, "about two months ago I ran an article on who the Gulch would be better without. This gent here was one." He blinked. "Next day I found the shop wrecked. He left a note sayin' the article was well-written from a lit'ry point of view, but the manners was kind of bad." He heaved his heavy shoulders regretfully. "Took me and my kid Bud, a week to fix up the type cases."

Larson glared at the "prisoner." "What've yuh got to say about that?"

"I'll pay for it," Bide Evans said. He smiled faintly, catching the look of surprise in Larson's eyes.

"If he does," put in Rivers quickly, "I'll withdraw the charge. The fight he put up at the Palace was worth it. Who won—Evans?"

"I did," said Bide.

"He didn't win that fight," interrupted a member of the "jury." "It was the other gent—who looks like him."

Suddenly, Bide understood what had happened. They meant to take his brother off the floor, but in the dark had made a mistake.

"Gents," he said, his gray eyes aglint. "Yuh're kind of mixed up. Yuh're even gettin' me confused. Soon I'll be thinkin' maybe I am who yuh say me to be."

"Enough of that!" snapped Larson. "Yuh're Matt Evans—no one else. That's all for yuh, Rivers."

The next man on the "stand" was Jim Squeeter. "Sheriff West came into the Star one day," he began, "lookin' for him." He pointed at Bide, then took his finger away fast. "The sheriff was set for trouble. Yuh could see it in the way his guns was swingin' loose.

"Evans was at the bar. Then he turns and sees the sheriff in the middle of the floor. His eyes are red and he ain't so steady on his pins. The sheriff says to him:

53

" 'Evans—last night a store was set afire and robbed. Yuh was seen comin' out of it. Are you comin' peaceful to the jug or do I have to gun-whip yuh?' "

Shadows gathered grayly around Bide's eyes. He didn't have to be told what was coming next.

"Evans didn't say nothin' for a minute," he continued, "but yuh could see a change come over him. He says to the sheriff, slow-like:

" 'Go 'way—I'm busy now.' But he stands there watchin' him.

"The sheriff gets red in the face and his arms start movin' back at the elbows. 'Maybe,' he says, 'I'll save the town some expense.'

"Evans ain't moved a muscle. He's standin' loose and easy there 'gainst the bar, like he's dreamin' of somethin'. Then he shakes his head, and he says to the sheriff:

" 'Yore move next—as they say in checkers—' "

Squeeter hesitated, licked his lips. The words came slower now.

"Well," he continued, "Sheriff West went swingin' for his guns—had 'em out, when he—" the little man nodded nervously at the 'prisoner,' "—went to work." His pace picked up. "The sheriff was no slouch when it came to guns, but the next minute he was crumblin' to the floor. He had fired, but the shots went into the sawdust.

"Evans stood there for a minute, then put his smokin' hoglegs back, shook his head sorrowful-like, and walked out." Squeeter shook his own head. "Never seen the like of it. The sheriff drew first, had his guns out, but it was Evans who remained standin'—"

"That's enough, Squeeter," said Larson. He looked down grimly at Bide. "Well—what do yuh say to that? Resistin' an officer of the law and killin' him?"

Bide Evans shook his head. This time he had nothing to say. He sat hunched in his chair and watched Squeeter scurry off like a rat for a hole. His chin went down on his chest.

"Bring the next witness in," he heard Larson call.

Coming to the Gulch, he had been grim and bitter. Now, he felt depressed. Listening to the testimony had done that to him. There was no question about it—Matt had a bad streak running through him.

Nevertheless, the doubt in his mind had grown. Nowhere had Matt shown himself to be a cold-blooded killer.

On the contrary, Matt fought cleanly with his fists and guns. If the latter's story were true, could Matt have fired two bullets into Symes' fallen body? Symes was an old, crippled man and obviously no match for Matt.

A gray-haired man passed him on the way to the 'stand.' When the latter turned and sat down, Bide's eyes widened; but he made no other gesture to show the surprise he felt.

"Tell the court, Farrell, what yore pardner and yuh told me," said Larson.

It was Ed Farrell, leathery-faced, thin. As he turned his faded blue eyes on the 'prisoner,' he gasped aloud:

"Bide! Am I seein' things?"

"Howdy, Ed," said the redheaded Texan.

A perplexed look was in the miner's eye. "I was wonderin' where yuh disappeared—"

"What do yuh mean, Farrell?" demanded Larson sharply.

"Why Ming and me was comin' into the Palace," replied the oldster, "when I saw Bide get socked on the jaw and go down. Then the lights went out, so we grabbed him and toted him out to the alley. I went for water and when I came back, he was gone. Ming said he just come to and walked away."

Bide gave vent to a short laugh. "There's yore answer, Larson," he said. "Yuh just picked up the wrong member of the Evans family."

"No we didn't!" fairly shouted Larson, reddening. He turned to Farrell. "Tell yore story."

Briefly, uncertainly now, the placer-miner told about Black Henry. Then, pointing to Bide, he described how the Texan saved him.

"It's his twin," cried Larson, exasperated. "They look alike."

"That's easy to find out," said Farrell suddenly. "In the shootin', Bide here got nicked. I fixed his bandage. Sure!" he cried abruptly. "There's the blood-stain on his sleeve.

A spare smile rolled a thin curve the length of Bide's lips. For the first time, doubt appeared in Sam Larson's face.

"Take yore shirt off, Evans," said the latter.

Bide rose and quickly peeled his shirt.

"There she be!" cried Farrell triumphantly. "Just like I told yuh. That's Bide Evans, all right."

A masked "juror" called out:

"Maybe we did make a mistake, Sam?"

The general store owner shook his shaggy head stubbornly. "I'm positive—" he began.

But no one heard his words. For the outside room was suddenly shaken by a burst of yelling, and the outspoken clatter of six guns. Then the door crashed open and screaming, shooting men plunged into the "courtroom."

Bide Evans was out of his chair and facing the door when the huge, black-bearded man led the way in. The latter saw him and roared his satisfaction.

"Matt!" he yelled. "C'mon out of here." The guns in his hairy hands opened up and the lights shattered out. His voice sounded over the rumble of Colt talk. "Boys, we're gettin' shut of these damn Vigilantes tonight. This way, Matt."

"Here I come, friend," yelled Bide.

Grinning briefly, the Texan was already moving. But not toward the door. He had grabbed Farrell and jerked him against the wall. "Let's get out of here, Ed," he whispered softly.

Jets of lurid flame lanced the room's darkness as Vigilantes and Hounds exchanged shots. Acrid fumes stifled the air. Savage cries beat above the gunfire. A deafening roar filled the place.

Hugging the wall, Bide snaked quickly along, Farrell following on his heels. He made a turn at the corner—and suddenly ran into a man. The latter was more startled than he and gasped aloud. Then Bide remembered Dan Rivers had been standing in this corner.

"This ought to give yuh a bang-up story for yore paper, Rivers," he told the printer.

Rivers gasped. "Who the devil are yuh? Bide or Matt?"

"Tell yuh tomorrer," replied Bide. "C'mon Ed." He reached the window that had been his goal, kicked out the glass and dived through.

Fresh air beat against him, then he cursed softly. He had landed on his hands and knees in a brush clump that raked his sore-bruised face. For a second, pain scored him like a barbed wire.

Ed Farrell came sailing down beside him. He helped the oldster up and together they made a circling run for it. Over his shoulder, the building he just quit looked like an abandoned warehouse.

They came out of the brush on the outskirts of the town

and passed the part-clay, part-wooden *juzgado*. Not far from it, across the road, Bide noticed a neat-looking, white painted little frame house with a garden.

While walking toward the town's center, Bide told Farrell that he'd had a fight with his brother and had knocked him down. That was why, he explained, the mistake had occurred.

"A mixup, for certain," commented the oldster. "But yore brother sure has his name on our claim. Found Ming. He told me he was konked near town and the paper stolen from him. When he came to, he rushed to the Claims Office, but found it already entered. He spent the next day tryin' to get folk to believe him. But who'd listen to a Chinee? No one—except Sam Larson. Then I spoke to Larson and he asked me to come to the trial."

"Well, yuh pick up yore pard, Ed," said Bide thoughtfully, "and get back to Dutch Diggin's. I'll see my brother to straighten out the claim business, and foller yuh out there tomorrer mornin'."

"Sure," said Farrell.

They parted in front of the hotel.

Idly Bide remembered that the stairs creaked in the same places the last time. The light was out in the corridor and the planks sounded hollow to his boots. A faint but recent odor of tobacco smoke sat in the dark hallway. He groped for his doorknob, pushed it in.

He brought up abruptly, stepped aside. Against the silhouette of the window, smoke clouds drifted. A match flared suddenly; and by its brief yellow cone, he saw the dark face of Tay Brown.

The match paled, went out. The gambler spoke softly: "It's all right, Bide Evans. Come in."

Nothing warned Bide of danger, no crawling feeling down the spine, no tightening of the stomach muscles. He stepped into the room and kicked the door shut with his heel. He stood with his back against the door, his eyes probing the obscurity.

"I came alone," Brown said, putting the cigarette to his mouth.

Bide said, "I'm listenin'."

"Sorry about the trial, Evans," declared the gambler. "But yuh can't blame us for the mistake. Never saw twins like yuh."

Bide asked, "Yuh heard Black Henry?"

57

"He made the same mistake the Committee made."

"All right," said the Texan. "What next?"

The gambler took his time. "I think yore brother called yuh, 'Sheriff'—in the saloon." His voice became inflected at the end; made a question.

"Yeah?"

"And then he said, 'come and get me,'" said Brown.

"I'm still listenin'," said Bide Evans softly.

"That was a Wanted poster yuh flashed in his face. 'Matt Evans. Wanted.' Wasn't it, Bide Evans?"

Bide wondered sharply at what happened to the poster. The last he had seen of it was a tight ball in Matt's hand. If Brown, he reflected, had the poster, or had seen it, he wouldn't be asking the question. Then six weary months flashed in his face. And something in him held, grew stronger. He shook his head slowly in the darkness and a rueful smile tugged at his lip corners.

"There's another question in yuh, Brown," he said. "Let's have that one, too."

Tay Brown's face showed grim behind the cigarette glow. "Yes," he said slowly. "The Committee don't think Matt Evans should be sheriff." He paused. "Would yuh take yore brother's place—for a short time, as sheriff? We'd be glad just to get him out of the Gulch. He has friends who might object if he disappeared. But with yuh around, they wouldn't know 'til too late."

"Yuh sound emptied out of questions, Brown," Bide said. "So I won't keep yuh. The answer is 'No.'"

A silence, somehow painful to the Texan, crowded the room. He had answered a cold, deliberate lie to Brown's questions. The reason? Not one but several. But he was sitting in a peculiar game. Cards were turning up that must have come from another deck.

"Guess I was wrong about yuh, Mr. Bide Evans," said Brown coldly. "Figgered yuh was on the same side as the rest of us."

"Maybe I am, friend," murmured Bide softly.

Brown crossed to the door and his voice came dry and empty to Bide.

"Maybe it would be a good idea if both brothers got out of town. Blood is thicker than water—but it spills just as easy." Then he was gone.

For a few moments Bide Evans remained motionless in the dark. Then he went to the window and found the

58

gambler's form receding down the street. It was late out there, the street emptying. As he stood there, a banner waved mockingly at him from the center of the town.

"Matt Evans for Sheriff," it said.

Smiling mirthlessly, he turned from the window, took the chair and propped it under the doorknob. Then he swung the bed into a corner—away from the window.

9. Counter Plan

EVENTS WERE spinning a fast and wicked pace around Bide Evans and his twin brother—even while Bide was still a prisoner of the Vigilantes. And further events were being hatched—that same night, which were intended to enmesh and destroy the newcomer to the Gulch.

For the tenth time that night, little Charley Oaks stumbled past the doors of the Star saloon. Noise swirled around him like the pungent tobacco clouds drifting through the room.

" 'Ray for Matt Evans," came out of his stubbled, moist chin. The banner strung over the bar echoed him.

He staggered that way but jostling shoulders shunted him over past the bar's end. He crashed into a table, knocking down the bottle on it, and fell into a chair.

" 'Ray," he cried feebly.

The lone occupant of the table swung up angrily, seized Charley Oaks by the shirt and sent him slamming head-long into the sawdust. Charley rolled over once, then slowly sat up, his stubble matted, his bleary eyes fumbling for his attacker. He found him sitting there, glaring at him.

"Shorry, Mr. Wurt," mumbled Charley. He picked himself up and made the bar. "Shay, Highpockets," he asked the bartender, "whatsa matter with Mr. Wurt t'night?"

The sallow-faced bartender, built high off the ground, with weepy sacs under eyes, shrugged his shoulders. "Don't know, Charley," he said. "Never seen the boss thataway. Looks kind of worried. Came in 'bout an hour ago actin' like he'd seen a ghost. He grabs a bottle and's been sittin' and drinkin' there alone by hisself."

Highpockets was right. Jim Wurt was a worried man. The thought of Matt's brother, and the tale of swift and sudden death to two of his men, told him by the third, troubled him.

He should have known that a note slipped under the door would do nothing but stimulate Bide Evans' curiosity. And now, he sorely regretted it.

The noise in the saloon suddenly ceased. Jim Wurt came around, listening. In a moment, Matt Evans' name was borne in. It was taken up by the crowd in the saloon, and the din became deafening.

The owner of the Star toyed with his empty glass. He should have felt pleased. It was what he had wanted and planned—and needed to make him top man in the Gulch. But somehow, it didn't bring the anticipated pleasure.

One of his men came looking for him on the run. Moe Wilson was pinched, scarred, nondescript.

"Boss," cried Wilson, "Matt's back!"

"No, he ain't!" snapped Wurt. His mood was ugly. "It's his twin brother yuh seen."

"Then maybe Matt's got two twin brothers," declared Wilson. "Because both of them were havin' a kind of debate with their fists in the Palace—"

Wurt pushed away from the table, his high forehead abruptly red. "Matt!" he cried, grabbing Wilson's arm.

"That ain't all, boss," said the other. "Just as I come away, I seen them Vigilantes goin' through the Palace windows."

Wurt's hand fell away and with it the blood from his forehead. "Vigilantes," he bit out grimly. "They're after Matt." Sitting down swiftly, he scribbled out a brief note and gave it to Wilson. "Back room, Moe."

Wurt watched his man swing through the crowd to a door at the other end of the room, then disappear beyond it.

"So the Vigilantes are holdin' court without Number Eight," he muttered grimly. "Sam Larson's work." His eyes shuttered as he added softly, "That's all, Mr. Larson."

He sat thus for ten minutes when his gaze happened to wander past the doors. It stopped suddenly, transfixed.

A redheaded, bruise-faced man stood there. One of his eyes was half-closed and purplish; and there was a slightly bewildered look about him.

"Matt Evans!" someone shouted.

The raucous, half-drunk crowd hailed the newly elected sheriff and hauled him to the bar for a drink. Then they fell back to let the frost-coated owner of the Star through.

"Congratulations, Sheriff," cried Jim Wurt, showing an open-faced smile and shaking the electee's hand.

"Thanks, Mr. Wurt," answered Matt Evans returning the same brand of smile.

"Have a drink with me," said Wurt, taking Matt by the arm. He led the latter to his table and behind an affable mask, clipped out: "Didn't I tell yuh not to come back till tomorrer!"

Matt shrugged his shoulders, grinned. "Got lonesome for the Gulch."

"What happened at the Palace?" demanded Wurt curtly.

"Met Bide, blast him!" muttered Matt, feeling his jaw. "He's got dynamite in that fist. First thing I know I'm in the alley back of the place and a Chinee is maulin' me."

"Alley!" gasped Wurt. "Wilson told me the Vigilantes came for yuh—so I sent Black Henry."

Matt Evans wrinkled his brows, then burst into a loud guffaw. "Ha!" he roared. "The Committee got Bide. Wait 'til Black Henry learns. Ha!"

Wurt reddened. "It ain't funny," he glowered. Then, "Yore brother came for yuh."

Matt said, "He told me." He grinned widely, showing his teeth. "But the badge's on my vest this time—not his."

Wurt rose. "Foller me into the back room, Matt," he said. "I want to talk to yuh."

It was almost six months since Jim Wurt had arrived in Hangman's Gulch. Six months in which his schemes had grown and matured under his facade of respectability—the frock coat and white, linen shirt; and the ownership of a saloon.

He was an ambitious, farsighted man; and thus, when he entered the Gulch, came alone. He brought with him no telltale followers. Matt Evans' subsequent arrival had been an unpleasant accident and surprise; but Matt had proven useful—and amenable. Later, of course, it became purely a business matter to supply the drinking wants of the hard-faced, tough-looking crew who made the Star their rendezvous.

Soon, the smallish man with the high forehead came to sit in the councils of the town. And when the Committee of Vigilantes was formed to combat the wave of killings

61

and robberies and claim-jumping that had broken out, Jim Wurt became Number Eight Vigilante.

Thus, while he took with one hand, he gave with the other. But his giving was dust in the eyes of the citizens of the Gulch, who watched with dismay the unchecked succession of crimes.

There had been but one minor flaw in the setup. Among the things Wurt wanted in the Gulch, beautiful Kate Larson inflamed his desires most. And because of Sam Larson's opposition, she seemed furthest from his grasp.

Tonight, he should have been jubilant. His man had become sheriff, and his claim-jumping scheme was working perfectly and filling his gold bags. Yet the unexpected appearance of Bide Evans was a grave threat to the continued success of his plans—and demanded immediate action.

Matt drew up a chair to the table instead of taking his usual place against the wall. Wurt noticed the change.

"When we're ready, Matt," he said shortly, "we'll sit out in the middle of the street together."

"Never mind that," muttered Matt. "I want to show you somethin'." He went into his pocket and fetched a wad of paper. He uncreased it and spread it flat on the table. It was the Wanted poster his brother had handed him. "Read it," he told Wurt, frowning.

"What?" repeated Matt. "This thing says I put two slugs into old man Symes. I told yuh how it happened."

"What's the difference?" said Wurt disinterestedly. "Yuh killed the old man—"

"Sure," said Matt. "I ain't denyin' it. But it was an accident. I ain't a cold-blooded killer."

Wurt's voice sounded as if his mind was on something else. "Yuh were drinkin' heavy that night, Matt. When yuh came up to my place, I had to drag yuh off the hoss."

"Yeah," grated Matt bitterly. "But I wasn't that drunk in the bank."

"What's the difference, Matt?" cried Wurt, annoyed. "What this means," nodding at the poster, "is we got to get rid of yore brother. I didn't have yuh elected sheriff for nothin'."

"Yeah," muttered Matt grimly, touching his bruised face. "I'll take care of Bide." Then his eyes showed a puzzled light and he shook his head. "It's kind of vague, that night. Maybe I did pull a gun on Symes. But I

62

could've sworn I didn't. 'Sides, the safe was cleaned and ten thousand dollars disappeared from it. Don't recollect touchin' that. Yuh know I never cared a hoot for money, Jim. If I took it—what happened to it?"

"Look, Matt," cried Wurt brusquely. "Let's forget this. It ain't important. Maybe yuh did take it—and spent it, or lost it."

"Maybe," said Matt slowly. He frowned. "There's somethin' about that night I ought to remember—but can't." He had found something in his pocket and now came out with it. He played with it in hand for a moment. Then he tossed the object onto the table. It gave off a metallic clink and glittered brightly under the candle. "Can't understand it," he grunted.

"What?" demanded Wurt, again showing annoyance.

"How in heck did my charm get into Symes' hand—when I lost it the week before?" cried Matt.

"Lost it?"

"Sure," said Matt. "Don't yuh remember? I asked yuh if yuh'd seen it. Thought I left it at yore place."

"Yuh're *loco,* Matt," declared Wurt. "I saw yuh wearin' it the day yuh killed Symes."

"I—" began Matt quickly; then he quit talking. He heaved his shoulders, then lazied back in the chair. He waited, knowing beforehand what Wurt was going to say.

"Yore brother has to go," Wurt said coldly.

"Looks like," muttered Matt. "He was always a lawman—tellin' me what to do. Even as kids. He was always right—and me wrong."

"Sure," he said. "I seen him take it out on yuh, Matt. Throwin' the holy family name in yore face—" He stopped abruptly, aware that he had taken the wrong track. Matt's eyes were glued on his face, and their shine was cold and bright.

"The Evans family, Wurt," said Matt slowly, putting out one word at a time, distinctly, separately, "was the first to settle in southwest Texas. We got one of the biggest spreads in the state and the toughest longhorns yuh ever seen—"

Wurt got excited. "I don't want to hear no more about yore family," he cried. "I'm tried of it. Just remember one shorthorn by the name of Matt Evans. And remember that I'm runnin' this outfit. I made yuh sheriff and yuh do as I say. Yore brother's—"

63

They suddenly heard the door open and close, and then a huge, bulking form loomed out of the darkness.

"Yuh got out?" grunted the newcomer.

Matt's face abruptly acquired a taunting smile. "Out, Black Henry?" he asked innocently. "Out of where?"

"What do yuh mean?" growled Black Henry.

"He means," cried Wurt, "the gent yuh went for is his twin brother."

"Brother!" cried the hairy man. Comprehension whipped across his broad, pocked face. "Say—I knew that *hombre's* voice sounded familiar! And that was Farrell then! Yore brother was the gent who spoiled my play this evenin' up at Dutch Diggin's."

"Yuh filed that jumped claim in my name?" demanded Matt suddenly.

Black Henry grinned widely, puckishly, in his beard. "Sure," he said. "Yuh said yuh was tired of not bein' a millionaire, so I fixed it for yuh. All yuh got to do ·is go out there and dig paydirt eighteen hours a day—"

"So that's what Bide meant," murmured Matt.

"Yuh dumb fool!" cried Wurt, eyes blazing. "Yuh tryin' to spoil everythin' now?"

"An *hombre's* got a right to file for his friend," grunted Black Henry. "And Matt's my friend—ain't he?" He gave Matt a mocking smile.

Wurt stood speechless with anger, his forehead bursting with blood.

"This ties Matt to yuh," he cried finally. "The Committee's lookin' for somethin' like this."

"The Vigilantes can't prove anythin' by that," declared Black Henry. "My name may be black, but my record's white. The official record." He laughed hoarsely.

"Besides," added Matt. "I'm the law in the Gulch now. They won't try anythin'. They made their last stab tonight when they grabbed Bide thinkin' it was me."

Wurt shook his head. "They won't stop tryin'," he declared. "I know 'em. And I don't want 'em thinkin' yuh two are tied together." His gaze swung around and snagged on the table. A grim smile crept under his beaked nose. Then he fetched a pocketknife out and cut a jagged, uneven strip from the Wanted poster. He tore the strip into tiny pieces.

Black Henry leaned on the table. "Hey!" he cried. "It's Matt. Wanted in Texas—"

"Sure it's Matt?" asked Wurt, in a gently hinting voice.

Black Henry looked up sharply. "Yuh mean——?"

"That's right," nodded Wurt. "His brother. Ain't it, Matt?"

For an instant, Matt stared at the smaller man. Then he laughed. "Yuh're smart, Jim," he said.

"What's goin' on here?" growled Black Henry.

Wurt explained briefly. "So tomorrer mornin'," he concluded, "yuh tell the claims clerk yuh made a mistake. 'Stead of Matt Evans, yuh meant Bide Evans. Then Dan Rivers'll run Matt off some fresh ones of these—and Matt'll plaster 'em up around town." He wore a satisfied look. "That ought to take care of Bide Evans, and the Committee."

"But I sent some boys to work that claim," protested Black Henry.

"Keep 'em there," said Wurt. "He'll never be able to turn it over to Farrell, and he'll never get around to usin' it himself."

Matt chuckled. "Bide's goin' to be kind of surprised," he said. "Claim-jumper and killer." He laughed again.

"We'll be shut of him now," said Wurt grimly.

"Maybe," said Matt slowly. He picked up the gold charm, dropped it into his pocket and went across the room. The other two heard his hand touch the doorknob.

"What'd he mean?" demanded Black Henry, when the door closed.

A queer light came and went in Wurt's eye. "Don't know," he said quietly. Then he added in a softly pushing voice. "Matt's been actin' kind of funny tonight. Got an idea he may decide to ride a straight trail from now on."

"What?" cried the big man. "Why the——"

"No," said Wurt. "Let's just wait and see if he does."

10. On the Move

DESCENDING the rickety stairs to the lobby next morning, Bide Evans found the hotelkeeper rocking in a chair. It swung to a halt as he hit the landing.

The nervous twitch was working back and forth.

"Leavin'?" asked the hotelkeeper. His voice scraped, like a file on edge.

"No," said Bide, his eyes touching the other's face, coldy.

"Need the room," said the hotelkeeper. Stitch marks showed red on the remaining half of his left ear.

"When I leave—yuh'll get it," said Bide. Evidently the other had learned of his error. His gaze caught and held the small man's shifting eyes. "Who were those three gents, last night?"

The hotelkeeper showed him a blank face, with lips kicking back into a wolfish grin. "Which men?"

Bide swung from him and went through the archway to the dining room. The Mexican waitress brought him a flashing smile with his breakfast.

"Caro mio," she told him. "You are a brave."

She was pretty he saw, with white even teeth, bold eyes and inviting red lips. *"Gracias,"* he said. "It is quiet here this mornin'," he added with quirking lips.

She matched his half-smile and added to it. *"Si. Pero* they are wicked *hombres* at the Star."

"So they came from Mr. Wurt's place," mused Bide. The waitress lingered a moment trying to catch his eye again, then went away with a saucy toss of her shapely shoulders. She stopped at the kitchen door, turning hopefully. But Bide was digesting the piece of news she had given him and his eyes weren't in the room. She shrugged and went inside.

When he had finished eating he went out to the street. It lay warm and quiet under the fresh early morning sun; and he stood a moment, eased against the hotel wall, tapering up a cigarette.

The town showed him a different shape than when he rode in with Ed Farrell. The night shadows had obscured its buildings and its spread was larger than he had suspected. Frame houses and buildings stood where he had only seen black shadows.

It was, he reflected, like the many other gold-field towns he had seen. It was big and full of life now; but as soon as the paydirt began to pan less than an ounce of gold dust a day, the town would suddenly contract. Overnight its inhabitants would vanish and its buildings empty. And his thoughts wandered around to Kate Larson, and he wondered what could keep her in a town like Hangman's Gulch.

He got the feel of the sun in his bones, then cut diagonally across the warming street in long, easy strides.

But even as he moved, the doubts of last night again surged up against him. Certain questions remained unanswered. Questions aroused by Matt's story; by the curious coincidence of Wurt's presence in the Gulch; his role of respectability; by the fact that the three gunnies came from his saloon; by the Vigilante trial—by everything that had happened since he had arrived.

His thoughts took a new drift. Although the men had come from the Star Saloon it didn't necessarily mean they were sent by Wurt. But it was a possibility which he had denied before.

If it were so, the note might also have been Wurt's. He recalled the animosity Wurt bore him—and assigned that as a reason if the premise was correct. Well—there were ways of finding out.

He shrugged his shoulders. But it was Matt he sought—not the suddenly respectable saloon owner. There was a course of action he pursued in involved circumstances like these. It was straight and to the point; for he was a man of direct action. Moreover, his body craved the bite and play of muscles in sweat and motion; and was impatient with delay. It was a weakness in him, he knew, but it was part of his makeup. At any rate, he had one or two calls to make first.

Kate Larson was behind the counter, when Bide Evans closed the door behind him. Her back was turned.

" 'Mornin', ma'm," Bide said, moving over. He saw her start and swing swiftly around. Then he felt her eyes reach out to him, touch his face, consider him.

"Who are you?" she asked. Her voice was without warmth. Yet he knew that it held great capacity for depth and emotion, and the knowledge troubled him.

He touched his vest. "Matt's wearin' the badge this mornin'," he said. She wasn't in a dress today. Riding trousers shaped her into a slender, boyish figure. And the pearl-gray shirt she wore was open at the throat, showing the soft, graceful lines in her neck. Her wide-set brown eyes were lighter than he had thought. Almost hazel.

"When you're through staring at me," she told him curtly, "perhaps you'll tell me what you want?"

Bide's eyes narrowed slightly; then a faint, amused smile slow-traveled his lean lips. This girl touched him to the quick, stirred his pulse. He found here something he had lost when he left the rolling plains of Texas.

"Sorry ma'm," he drawled. "Just dropped by for a box of cartridges—a .45 Colt. You were kind of in a rush last night, so I figgered I'd maybe better come back this mornin'."

A deep flush stained her cheeks. "You're not Matt?" Her eyes held uncertainty.

"Bide Evans, ma'm. Matt's my brother."

"You—were here last night?" she asked, troubled. When he nodded, she put him another question: "And then you fought with your brother in the Palace?"

Again he nodded. "Matt and I always been scrappin' —since we were youngsters."

"He told me about you, once," she said unexpectedly. "About the Evanses—and their land and their herds." A curious, soft look sat deep in her eyes.

Surprise stirred in Bide. "Matt told yuh about the Evanses?" he asked. Once more Matt was showing him a new side.

"Yes," she replied. "He sounded proud—but that was when he first came here." Anger was a faint note in her voice. "He's done nothing since to justify that pride."

"We were a proud family," he murmured.

"You look alike," she said. Then hesitating: "But— your eyes are different."

He nodded. "Gray. Matt's are green—maybe one purple one this mornin'."

For the first time since he entered the store, a smile played on Kate's face. "My father came home angry, last night," she said. "Angry and puzzled, I think."

Bide said, "There's been one question I been wantin' to ask yuh since last night."

Her eyes met his and he felt an almost physical shock in the contact.

"What?" she asked quietly.

He made a lean, loose shape in the room, yet there was a suggestion of power and pride in him. But instead of asking, he told her, for the impression was strong in him.

"Yuh ain't made for a town like this, Kate," he said, using her first name unconsciously; nor did she seem aware of it. "Yuh belong on a good hoss, ridin' tall grass country, with Texas winds blowin' through yore brown hair and in yore face. This town is gold-mad, like every other town in California. And the people here are kind of *loco* with it. It ain't fit air for a person to breathe—for yuh." He smiled faintly. "I reckon yuh just don't belong here, Kate."

He had made an impression upon her. She stood there, her eyes locked on his lean face, color strangely absent from her cheeks, her red lips slightly parted.

Then the moment was gone, and the curious light he had seen kindled deep in her eyes, gone with it. Blood flashed in her face and her glance was smileless. Her voice held the same quality.

"I hardly see how it concerns you," she said.

Bide flushed. "Sorry," he said. "I—"

"Get 'em lifted, Evans!" the voice sprang harsh from the end of the counter. Bide wheeled, found himself staring into the muzzle of a big Colt .44. Behind the gun was grim, shaggy-headed Sam Larson. Bide's lips flattened. He had been wool-gathering and had not heard Kate's father come through the door at the side.

"Yuh're makin' a mistake, Larson," he said, raising his arms slowly.

"This is Bide Evans, Father," Kate put in. "Matt's brother."

For a moment, Larson glared at him. Reluctantly, then, he lowered his gun.

"Yore temper's goin' to lead yuh to trouble, Larson," Bide pointed out coldly, hauling down his arms. "Better not try that against Matt. He's got a bigger temper—and besides, he's lawman in the Gulch now." It was his own temper talking, he realized.

Sam Larson remained grim-faced. And the words he put out were hot and vehement: "I don't want no traffic with the Evans family—yuh or yore brother! Get out of the store and stay out! And tell yore brother the same." He added, "It would be a good thing if both of yuh left the Gulch."

Bide tensed and the call of action flared wildly through his muscles. He made a tough, hard figure haunched there with the threat of violence sitting him. Then out of the corner of his eye, he caught Kate's face abruptly gone white; and the harshness went out of him.

"Maybe yuh and yore Vigilantes know somethin' about

the note I got," he said. "And the three gents who were worried about my health." If Bide thought to surprise Larson, he was doomed to disappointment, for the latter's face remained unmoved.

"Get out," the store owner cried.

Bide showed father and daughter a thin, windless smile, then turned and quit the store.

He turned down the street and halted in front of Dan Rivers' Printing Shop. He went in.

The shop looked like the printer, Bide thought, big, disorderly and not especially clean. Behind a railing stood a fairly large press which a kid was washing down. A shelf beside it was loaded heavily with black-stained ink tins. Across from the press were two or three type cases; and throughout the shop, papers lay scattered.

A rolltop desk in the corner had concealed Dan Rivers' bulk until now. He rose and shifted it to the rail. His glance, owlish and wide, angled from Bide's vest to his face.

"Yuh're Bide Evans," he murmured.

Bide nodded. "What's the bill, Rivers?" If asked to explain his purpose in paying his brother's debts, Bide might have been stumped for a minute, then answered, "Family pride." But he wouldn't have been certain.

Rivers' eyes lay thoughtful in his face. He unhooked the pencil stub from behind his ear and fooled with it. "It don't add up," he said. "What was Black Henry doin' there last night?"

"Complete surprise to me," said Bide.

For a second, the printer stared at him from lidded eyes. Then Rivers stuck his pencil back into place. "Reckon maybe I'll try collectin' from the sheriff." His voice had lost its friendliness.

Bide's cheeks pulled in and his lips lost their bantering shine. Then his shoulders moved up and down in a shrug. "Got a piece of news for yore paper, Rivers," he said, and watched the embers of interest glow in the printer's eyes.

Rivers' flabby jowls moved with his words. "I don't turn down news that's of interest to the public, Evans— no matter who it's from."

"Yuh can write in that paper of yores," said Bide evenly, "that Matt Evans is goin' to resign his office and leave the Gulch."

70

Rivers blinked at him. "When?"

"Soon," Bide said. "Soon."

The printer watched the Texan leave his shop, cut into the dust and stride off. He kept watching until Bide Evans walked out of his angle of vision. It was a look of perplexity he turned on his son at the press.

"Bud," he said, "there's somethin' goin' on in this town whose drift I don't exactly get. But whatever it is, I got the feel of gun powder in my bones. Somethin' goin' to pop—and pop damn soon."

Bide Evans stopped by at the stable to pick up his black.

The greasy hostler with his straw hat pulled over his eyes watched Bide cinch the saddle straps.

"Spittin' image," Bide heard him mutter. Then aloud, "Leavin'?"

Bide said, "Reckon," and swung up into leather. He threw the hostler a silver and shook his horse down the street.

"Spittin' image," murmured the hostler after him. He poked a dirty finger under the straw and scratched his head. Then he called to his stable boy.

Bide left the Gulch the way he came, from the east side of the town. He knew it was impossible for him to shoot his own brother and did not want to be put in the way of doing it. Of Matt he had his doubts; but he, Bide, always played the game according to his own lights and not anyone else's.

A pressure in the small of his back told Bide that eyes had watched him go—and that soon word would get around that he had pulled town. That was all right, too.

He took the east trail along the stream. Soon Hangman's Gulch dimmed off behind him, the buildings and stores growing small and vague. When he rounded the bend that took him completely out of sight of town, he angled off sharply toward the slope on the left—and cut back.

He went up among the jack-pines and oaks, picking his way in a diagonal line with the heating sun on his back. He worked the horse steadily until below him, on his left, the housetops of the Gulch showed between the trees, and the stream lay thin and gleaming.

He rode on for a short time, then dipped down toward the town. The day was showing a bright surface, but the sun was behind him and not sufficiently strong under the tree shadows to narrow his eyes and furrow his brow.

The habits of his life had trained Bide Evans to be observant and critical. That was why he was faintly disturbed now. There were elements in this situation which whispered softly for attention. He had heard the low voice of trouble before, and the way it sifted ominously through the streets of the Gulch, and in the glances men gave each other, and in the subtle undercurrent of their conversation, was enough for him. It was like a pattern he had seen traced many times in the past—traced in gunsmoke and blood, in deceit and treachery and killings. And his brother was there in the center of it.

Yet his thoughts were suddenly taking a new course. If certain things were true—simple things, like Matt's story of the killing of Symes, then other things became equally true, such as the possibility that Matt hadn't killed Symes at all.

These were the considerations which Bide turned over in his mind as he left the slope, cut across a clearing and came into sight of his destination—the Gulch *juzgado*.

11. Visitor's Day

THE STREAM which poured through the Gulch narrowed to a thin, shallow trickle as it passed the rear of the part-clay, part-wooden structure whose bars fixed a crisscross pattern on all its windows.

Bide dismounted and cautiously led the big black across the stream, then along the side of the jail. There was a rear door, but it seemed locked. It was the last building at this end of the town and to Bide's right lay a stretch of brush, piney country.

He came to a halt near the corner of the jail, shed his sombrero and snapped a quick look over the end window jamb. His brother was alone in the office. Restoring his hat, Bide left his horse standing there, moving quietly

72

around to the front, and stepped boldly through the open door.

"Yuh comin', Matt?"

Matt Evans was seated at a battered, rolltop desk. At the sound of the voice, he wheeled fast, and went smoking for his guns. He pulled up as he faced into the Colt in Bide's hand. He grimaced, and fell back into the chair, from which he had half-risen.

"Damn yuh," he growled.

Bide surveyed his brother briefly in the bright morning light. He saw nothing there he hadn't seen the previous night, except the slightly blackened eye. Possibly the taint of dissipated living was etched more clearly; that was all.

"Toss me the badge, Matt," he said.

Matt scowled at him. "What's the idea?"

"The Vigilantes made a mistake once," Bide replied. "I won't be takin' any chances when yuh and me ride out of the Gulch together."

His brother suddenly grinned, wickedly. "Yuh outfoxed yoreself last night, brother," he declared.

Bide said, "The badge, Matt."

The grin rolled off Matt's face. He shook his head. "No," he said.

Bide wiggled his gun. "Get up," he told his brother, his voice solid, hard. "And drop yore gun belt." His lips were flat against his teeth, and his eyes slate gray on Matt's face. For a brief instant there was a clash of wills, then Matt's eyes dropped away. Reluctantly, Matt rose, undid the belt buckle and let the belt slide to the floor.

"An Evans shoot an Evans?" he asked bitterly.

"If necessary," said Bide softly—lying. He moved forward, hooked his boot toe into the fallen gun belt and kicked it aside. Then, carefully, he slipped the star from Matt's vest and stuck it on his own.

"Well—what's next?" growled Matt.

Once more a faint pang of sympathy touched Bide unexpectedly. By some perverse trick of Fate his brother had been endowed with a bad streak. Otherwise they were pretty much alike—and not only in appearance. For a moment, a puzzled frown came to sit on Bide's forehead. In the drift and tide of his days, he had met up with a score of killers—dissolute men, thoroughly evil. He could have sworn Matt did not belong to that tribe. Yet the evidence of Symes' killing was too strong to deny.

And there were other things, here in Hangman's Gulch.

"Before we go," Bide said, "I want yuh to make out a bill of sale to Ed Farrell and Ming Foy on the claim at Dutch Diggin's—the one yuh didn't know anythin' about."

Matt laughed unexpectedly. "Sure," he said. "Be glad to do it for yuh, brother. It was all a mistake—the whole thing." He sat down promptly, scribbled off some words on a paper and handed it to Bide.

Bide glanced at the paper, nodded, then eyed Matt curiously. There was something in this acquiescence which disturbed him. It was too easily gotten.

"Yore friend, Black Henry—" he began.

"No friend of mine," growled Matt.

"Maybe that's why he called yuh at the Vigilante trial—huh, Matt?" snapped Bide. A faint, unreasoning anger whipped through him. His brother had spoken quickly, like the reaction of a finger to a hot stove. It had sounded like the truth. Yet it couldn't be.

"Mistake," said Matt.

Bide's annoyance increased. He could feel the lie in this; just as he felt the truth in the other. But together they didn't make sense. His eyes were narrow as he drove words like bullets at his brother.

"Just like the mistake yuh made with Symes—huh!"

"Yeah!" cried Matt, anger riding a rough wave across his face. "It was a mistake—and an accident!" he fairly yelled. "And I didn't gun the old man. Why should I—after he was dead?"

Bide breathed heavily and the imps of temper danced remotely in his eyes. "Let's settle this once and for all," he snapped. "Sit down, Matt." He pulled up a chair ten feet away from his brother. He sat with his back to the door and let his gun hand sag against the armrest. He searched Matt's face but found nothing in it—nothing but resentment.

There were such obvious discrepancies between the story his brother was telling and the story as he read it in Symes' office, that he could not be satisfied until the two were reconciled.

"Can yuh prove yuh lost yore gold charm a week before Symes died?" he demanded.

Matt hesitated a moment. "No," he answered, finally.

74

"What did yuh do with the money yuh took?" Bide asked.

Matt frowned, then flared. "I didn't take any money! How could I when the safe was locked?"

A cold chill went crawling down Bide's spine. "Locked?" he cried. "Why didn't yuh tell me that last night?"

"Just remembered Symes clicked the combination shut on the safe when I came in," cried Matt, glaring at him.

"Yuh're lyin' again," cried Bide.

"Yuh can go to hell!" yelled Matt.

Bide flushed, the blood whipping his face like pelting rain. He rose to his feet. "I don't know why I'm botherin' here with yuh. Yore whole story's a lie from beginnin' to end. 'Cause if the safe was locked, yuh didn't put them two slugs into Symes—and he was alive when yuh left him."

Matt's anger had equaled his own and the latter was on his feet now too—rigid, boiling. Then suddenly Matt's face underwent a change. The rage simmered off and a slow, dawning light came to his eyes. He spoke words slowly, and they seemed to come from all the way down in him.

"Yuh mean," he said, "maybe I didn't kill him?"

Bide caught the change and felt the chill again. He repeated a question he had put before. "Yuh were alone with Symes?"

"Yeah," said Matt.

"I found a set of hoofprints behind the bank made that night," said Bide.

"Huh?"

"C'mon," said Bide, suddenly impatient. "Let's get movin'."

"I don't think I'm goin'," drawled Matt abruptly, triumphantly.

A warning signal flagged Bide, but for once his instinct was late. He had begun to wheel, when a familiar voice rapped out behind him.

"Reach, Bide Evans."

Bide froze, then slowly lifted his arms. Out of the corner of his eyes he caught the frock-coated form of Jim Wurt stepping into the office. The smallish man had a small black derringer in his right hand.

"Sure glad to see yuh, Jim," called Matt. He moved

75

up, relieved Bide of his guns and threw them on the desk. He took off the badge and restored it to his own vest. Then he picked his belt off the floor and buckled it on.

"I wouldn't have known the difference between yuh, Matt," said Wurt, coming around, "if yore brother hadn't fixed yore eye."

"He fixed my eye," said Matt, the grin wearing off. "But now I'm on the fixin' end."

Bide's glance swung between them like a pendulum. Wurt was standing on his right and Matt directly in front of him at the desk. His eyelids drew together as his gaze finally settled on Wurt.

"So yuh two ain't together?" he said.

"Not at all," declared Wurt smoothly. "Just came in to offer my congratulations to the sheriff. Saw him in trouble—" He lifted his well-groomed shoulders and let them fall.

"Mighty sudden interest yuh're displayin' in Matt—and law and order," said Bide. "Reckon it came with them fancy clothes." His voice twisted against the other with the bite of sarcasm in it.

Wurt flushed deeply and he wet his lips with his tongue. But he maintained control over his voice. "I told yuh before how I stand, Evans," he said. "What happened in Texas ain't no worry of mine. Matt and I have no reason to be together."

"Yeah," drawled Bide. " 'Cept that yuh ran his election campaign for him—after gettin' him out of town. Yuh knew the Vigilantes would never let him run. So now yuh came to collect—huh?"

It was a guess, backed by sudden intuition, by the pattern this situation was tracing and by knowledge of the men involved. And watching Wurt's face through narrowing eyes, told him it was a good guess.

Wurt cast a quick, enigmatic glance at Matt. "Well—" he began.

"He's fishin'," Matt cut in.

"In a cesspool," said Bide quickly, deliberately trying to crack through Jim Wurt's armor. He was almost certain there was something between these two, and he was deeply interested in it.

"Damn yuh!" cried Wurt, blood crowding the veins in his neck. He brought up the gun in his hand.

"Take it easy, Jim," Matt cried, laughing bluntly, waving his heavy Colt at him. But there was a curious stiffness in his voice. It hooked Wurt's attention; and then he let the derringer fall back. "Can't yuh see he's baitin' yuh?" added Matt.

"No I ain't, Matt," said Bide quickly. "Did yore friend Jim tell yuh he pushed a note under my door last night sayin' the air in the Gulch was kind of unhealthy for me—and then sent three gents to prove it?" Slit, his eyes were tight on Wurt's face. Already stained red, it acquired a deeper hue. But Wurt's black eyes remained unreadable. Bide threw his glance swiftly at his brother and saw surprise spring to his features.

Bide paid out a grudging admiration to Wurt. For the latter had regained his self-possession and was considering him with composure. Then the saloon owner turned lifted eyebrows on Matt and said casually, "I think yore brother is *loco,* Sheriff. Maybe he ought to be locked up."

A wilting smile ran off Bide's lean lips. Wurt wasn't asking Matt—he was telling him. This was confirmation of his guess; and it also indicated where his brother stood in the relationship.

"Yeah," declared Matt. "Reckon I ought to keep him locked up for a while—till he cools off."

"What's the charge, Sheriff?" asked Bide, using sarcasm again.

Matt laughed in his face. "Yuh got me, brother," he said mockingly. "But while yuh're in there—" he threw his thumb over his shoulder at a door which obviously led to the cells, "—I'll figger somethin' out. Don't fret. Maybe resistin' arrest, or—"

"Yuh mean like Sheriff West?" said Bide softly. He saw the sardonic gleam fade in Matt's eyes. "Speakin' to some Vigilantes," he drawled, "and they told me they wasn't sure of gettin' the sheriff's cooperation. So I told Rivers this mornin', he could say in his paper that Matt Evans is leavin' the Gulch."

"Yeah," said Matt, suddenly smiling again. "Rivers told me. So I told him yuh were kind of confused—that it was yoreself yuh meant. And another thing—I pay my own bills."

Bide shrugged his shoulders. "Good idea—about the bills, I mean." An idea struck him. "Wurt," he said casually. "Maybe I'm wrong about yuh and Matt here." He hesitated, and the idea grew stronger in him. "But yuh and him ran together for a time, back in Dudley."

"So what?"

"Nothin'," replied Bide gently. " 'Cept I never asked yuh where you were—the night Symes was killed."

The opaque depth of Wurt's black eyes seemed to lose focus and grow lighter. "Why?" he asked.

"Nothin'," said Bide slowly. "But the one who plugged Symes made a little mistake."

Just then, Bide heard the faint rumble of hoofs, approaching from the west. He knew he had to move fast if he was going to get out. So he took a chance, wondering whether his brother would use his gun.

He twisted abruptly and broke the distance between him and Wurt in a single leap. It carried him to Wurt's left, putting the latter between Matt and himself. Before the smallish man could bring his derringer up, Bide clamped his hand on Wurt's shoulder and using it as a pivot, whipped behind him. A lead pellet tugged at his sleeve before he heard the echo of a gun roaring in back of him.

Instantly hugging Wurt to him and seizing the latter's gunhand, which waved wildly about, in a grip of steel, Bide fell back toward the door with Wurt writhing in his grasp.

A wisp of smoke was curling from the Colt in Matt's fist, and there was a savage, fighting gleam in his eyes. Matt had moved forward with the shot, but now he came to an abrupt halt as a bullet plowed the planks at his feet.

Bide had managed to fasten his hand over Wurt's and had squeezed the latter's trigger finger. He smiled thinly, grimly, as he continued backward, using Wurt as a shield.

Jim Wurt was no longer a well-groomed man. His hair was disheveled, his frock coat twisted. His face was livid with hatred as he lay helpless in Bide's grasp, trembling with the intensity of his outraged emotions.

"Get him, Matt," he shrieked. "Get the damned son!"

"Hold him still," cried Matt. "Turn him around."

Bide laughed in his throat. For a moment he would have sworn he had seen a glint of sardonic humor in Matt's eyes.

"Throw yore gun here—at my feet, Matt," Bide cried. His right hand now fitted like an iron glove over Wurt's gun hand, solid, hard. He laid a shot across his brother's

78

chest to show he meant business. But time was running out. Those hoofbeats were nearer now and he saw that Matt had heard them. Slowly, face flushed, wicked-looking, Matt complied.

"Now the other one," ordered Bide. When the second gun clattered near his feet, he rapped out, "Yuh're comin' with me, Matt."

Matt shook his head slowly and showed Bide a wide, mocking smile. "Not today, brother," he said.

Grim words rose to Bide's lips, but the beat of those nearing hoofbeats was ominous and loud in his ears. Instead, he said, "I'll be back." Then he wrenched the derringer from Wurt's hand and with his knee shoved the one-time rustler sprawling in Matt's direction.

Tossing the little black gun over his shoulder, Bide stooped fast, snatched the Colts off the floor, threw a warning shot across the room and wheeled out of the jail.

12. Shifting Plays

BIDE EVANS hit the dust running. As he made the jail's corner his eyes caught a group of horsemen entering the clear stretch of trail between the brush and the jail. Even in the distance, he could make out the huge bulk of Black Henry. He triggered two shots in that direction, jammed the Colts into holsters and went sailing into leather.

The long-legged black, with only the stiffness worked out of him by the morning's ride, lit out fast when spur steel raked his sides. The animal took the stream in its stride and flashed across the clearing behind the jail.

Gun echoes set up an insistent clamor and Bide felt bullets begin to hum around him with a steely tune. He threw a look over his shoulder. His two shots had evidently halted and dispersed the group of horsemen for a moment. But now, with Matt standing there gesticulating fiercely and Wurt beside him firing a gun like a madman, Black Henry and his men were after him.

It was hardly likely, Bide thought briefly, as he hunched

79

low in the saddle, that Black Henry had recognized him in the distance, although the former's size made him easily identifiable. That meant that Black Henry was following Matt's direction in this; which proved that Matt had lied when he denied being friendly with the big, black-bearded man. But where did Wurt stand—if at all—in relation to Black Henry?

He suddenly gave up his thinking as shouts and shots fell clearly around him. A tight grin, cut a severe slice out of his lips and he set up a zigzagging, curvetting course; until he hit timber. Here, under the shadows of low-spreading oaks, he angled sharply to the east. The cries of pursuit swelled up to his rear and he chopped up the trail, cutting and angling, and working his horse hard, but still keeping generally eastward.

Finally the grim lines eased off his face as the sounds behind him fell away, and then were swallowed up by silence. He continued up the sloping side of the Gulch for a time and then halted to give the black a breather.

It was, he knew, no more than four or five miles back to the bend of the stream—and from there a short distance to Dutch Diggings. He rode a comfortable pace listening to the low-pitched gurgle the down yonder water made, and to the way the breeze faintly rustled the pine tops.

The situation with Matt had hardened into a clean-cut, arbitrary picture. Either Matt's story was a complete falsehood and Matt guilty as hell; or, Matt was telling the truth, which meant he was entirely innocent of Symes' death.

For an instant, hope shot through Bide. Luke Evans was bent and battered; Matt's innocence would permit the old man to raise his whitened head and spend his declining years in peace and dignity.

Bide laid the hope aside as he recalled Matt's confession. Yet other facts were equally important. If he assumed that his brother's story was true: the charm lost and the safe locked; it would mean, simply, that Matt had erred in believing Symes dead. Symes had merely been unconscious.

It would mean that after Matt had left the bank, someone else had entered, possibly the man whose horse stood at the bank's back window, forced the reviving banker to open the safe and then cold-bloodedly shot him. Then the killer had placed Matt's charm in Symes' hand and departed, assured that blame would fall on Matt Evans' head.

Yet this explanation was so obvious that Bide was chary of it. It would mean that his six-month chase had been for nothing; that he had been blinded by overt evidence and his own family pride; that his customary methodic habits had been swept aside by prejudice.

Matt may have been bad, but he was not a cold-blooded killer. Of that Bide was certain. Then Matt could have shot Symes in a fit of temper? But there was his story. He had pushed Symes and the banker fell on his head. The whole question then turned on whether Matt was lying—which was where he had started.

The circle was complete in Bide's mind when he set his black down near the bend in the stream. The sun had by now climbed to the top of the sky and sat there, big and warm. Two long-legged cranes, gray and dappled against the water, rose in abrupt flight and wheeled off. A hawk plummeted down out of a lazy overhead drift and came up with water glistening on its wings, and a silvery fin gleaming from its beak.

Bide felt a sudden longing for the sweeping plains and rolling herds of Texas. Perhaps that was why he was thinking of Kate Larson and the calm of her hazel eyes, when the clatter of hoofs and querulous pitch of voices coming down the trail smote his ears.

He pulled over and waited behind a tree. Circumstances of the past twenty-four hours had made a careful man of him. In a moment a burro hove in sight. A pig-tailed Chinese in a mandarin costume, led the animal, and astride it sat a thin, wiry miner. Their gesticulations might have been amusing to Bide, except that the rider had a bloodied bandage tied around his head—and that it was Ed Farrell.

"What happened, Ed?" demanded Bide, leaving the tree.

"Bide!" yelled Farrell, his face lighting up. "Plenty," he said, answering the question. "But first meet up with my pard, Ming Foy. Ming, this is Bide Evans."

The Oriental bowed gravely. "I am grateful," he said, "to meet the savior of my friend." Then he stood erect, his pigtail swaying from underneath the black mandarin hat, the bright orange blouse he wore, shining brilliantly in the sun. His age was indeterminate, for his yellowish face was smooth and unwrinkled, and his slanting, black eyes, bright.

"Howdy," said Bide nodding, smiling faintly at the courteous manner and speech. It was, he thought, a little strange for a white man and yellow to be partners. He had seen many Chinese in the gold camps and towns, but they were the cooks and launderers, and placer miners among themselves—never the partners of whites. Yet they had a reputation for honesty and he saw no reason against a partnership. Moreover, Ming Foy had a solid and substantial look that he liked.

Briefly, the gray-haired miner told the story. He and Ming had returned to Dutch Diggings the night before and in the morning had begun to work their claim.

"Then two gents come ridin' up," continued Farrell, "and tell us to get off Matt Evans' claim. Said they was hired to work it. I tried to get 'em to wait till yuh came— and told 'em why. They laughed and told us to get movin'. So I went for my rifle, but they had the jump on us." He shrugged his thin shoulders.

Shadows darkened momentarily around Bide's deep-set eyes and his lips thinned. He went into his pocket and fetched the paper Matt had given him. Without comment he handed it to the miner.

Farrell's blue eyes gleamed and he thrust the note at Ming. "Told yuh," he cried, "he'd get it back for us."

Ming looked at it, then lifted his gaze to Bide. "It is written," he said, "that a true friend is worth twice his weight in gold."

"Let's go back," cried Farrell eagerly.

"Wait," said Bide, his eyes suddenly twinkling. "I got an idea." In a few words, he explained what he had in mind. It drew chuckles from Farrell and sober assent from Ming.

"Justice is a rare fruit," observed the latter. "When it ripens and falls, good people are stricken dumb with admiration."

"In the meantime, Ed," said Bide. "You can ride to town and show the note to the claims clerk. There'll be plenty of time, and we'll wait for yuh at the trail."

Back at the *juzgado* at Hangman's Gulch, when Bide Evans left in such a hurry, Jim Wurt gave a demonstration of how an angry man acts.

82

After he picked his derringer up on the run and emptied its chambers at the back of the fleeing horseman with no apparent results he slammed it to the dust and fell to cursing and swearing. His face boiled with blood and he foamed at the mouth. And if the respectable citizens of the Gulch had seen their colleague, they might have wondered. For Jim Wurt looked anything but respectable.

"Take it easy, Jim," said Matt, watching the other with a kind of curiosity. "Yuh're actin' more scared than angry."

It was a shrewd observation, for it abruptly wrung the rage out of Wurt. He stooped for his gun and was slow in picking it up. But when he came erect, all vestiges of the emotional storm he had passed through, had vanished from his face.

He straightened his frock coat, adjusted his tie and combed his black hair smooth. Once more he became Jim Wurt, respected citizen and saloon owner of Hangman's Gulch. It was an amazing metamorphosis, but Matt Evans was not impressed; he had seen it before. They went inside.

"Noticed yuh weren't shootin', Matt?" Wurt said briefly.

"Yeah," muttered Matt, his brow contracting. "First place, I don't shoot men in the back. And in the second place," his voice slowed, "Bide's an Evans."

"He'd have shot yuh!" snapped Wurt, venom laying exposed in his eye.

Matt considered Wurt with narrowing attention. "Maybe," he said. Then he added, "He said maybe I didn't kill Symes."

"No?" Wurt's voice became politely disinterested. It said he was weary of discussing past history.

"Found hoofprints behind the bank," said Matt. His gaze was on the wall now, therefore he did not see Wurt start suddenly.

"Well," demanded Wurt evenly. "Did he trace 'em?"

Matt shrugged his shoulders. "Reckon not if he came after me," he said. "But if the killer made a mistake—"

"Yeah?" Wurt's voice was hardly a question.

"If I didn't kill Symes like I figgered I did," said Matt abruptly, "then I was framed."

Wurt covered a yawn and rose. "Yore brother's got to go, Matt," he said brusquely. "He's in my way here. If yuh don't want to do it, I'll turn the job over to Black Henry—and maybe get myself a new sheriff."

83

Matt gave him intent consideration, then his expression lightened. "I'll play the game, Jim. 'Course, if Bide finds I was framed—he'll clear out anyhow."

"Yore brother is nobody's fool, Matt," said Wurt earnestly. "He suspects we're together and maybe is tryin' to break up our play. But he can't do it."

"No," agreed Matt. "Not with that poster Rivers is printin' up. He can't come near the Gulch."

Wurt stood on the threshold. "If Black Henry brings him back," he said, "keep him here till I—we decide what to do with him."

"All right," said Matt. Then he added softly, "Say Jim—" Wurt swung back, eyebrows arched. "Did yuh send three of the boys after Bide?"

For an instant Wurt glared at the newly elected sheriff, then without answering went abruptly out of the jail office and strode down the street. There was a look on this smallish man's face that boded no good for someone.

Jim Wurt brushed an imaginary speck of dust off his shoulder, ran a finger along his mustache to bring out the shine, and entered Sam Larson's general store.

Kate Larson was standing near one of the windows. Wurt darted a quick, slanting glance around the store. It was empty, save for the girl.

"Good mornin', Kate," he said.

"Good morning, Mr. Wurt," she said pointedly, emphasizing the word "Mr."

"Kate," he insisted, flushing. "We been friends for a long time. Why can't yuh call me 'Jim'?" He lowered his voice. "Is it yore father?"

"My father has nothing to do with it," she said, her eyes cool, distant.

Wurt felt a stab of bitterness. But there was a hard substance to this man—part of his fierce, driving ambition, and he had to know.

"Then what's the reason?" he asked evenly. But his eyes betrayed him.

She shrugged her shapely shoulders and her voice, like her eyes, seemed remote. "I don't know," she said. "I've never thought about it."

It seemed like a faint hope to Wurt and he clutched at it desperately. "Yuh mean maybe—" he began, when she interrupted him.

"Have you ever been to Texas, Mr. Wurt?" she asked unexpectedly.

If he was surprised, his face betrayed no sign. But an intent ear might have heard his voice harden. "Why?"

"I heard," she said, and the faraway look was again in her face, "that there's grass for miles, and great herds—"

"Who's been tellin' yuh stories about Texas?" His voice was almost harsh. "Was it Matt Evans?"

She gazed at him a moment, then shook her head slightly. "No," she said. "His brother."

This time Wurt showed his amazement. His mouth fell open and his eyes widened. Then he snapped his lips shut, almost with a snarl. "That killer?" Somehow, he managed to get the proper mixture of loathing, surprise, dismay in those two words.

Kate Larson's hand flew to her throat and her eyes clouded. "Killer?" she asked in a small, oddly flat tone.

Wurt disguised the pleasure he got in telling her. "Sure," he said. "Stuck up a bank, robbed it and shot the banker."

"Are you certain?" Her voice was low, husky.

"Yeah," growled Wurt; but the pleasure was somehow gone. "Rivers is printin' a Wanted poster on Bide Evans right now. Just saw a copy."

Kate Larson turned from him and looked cut of the window. They were standing like that when a harsh voice cut across the room. Wurt turned quickly and saw Sam Larson storming over to them.

"Kate," ordered the shaggy-headed man sharply. "Leave us for a minute."

His daughter left them and went out the front door. Had they watched, they would have seen her walk down two stores and enter Dan Rivers' Printing Shop.

Jim Wurt spoke first. Having been on the defensive so many years of his life, he knew the advantage of the offensive.

"Yuh're takin' a lot on yore own shoulders, Larson," he said. "Don't forget, yuh ain't runnin' the Gulch."

"What do yuh mean?" demanded the big-boned storekeeper.

"Yuh know what I mean," cried Wurt, with a pretended indignation. "There was a meetin' of the Committee last night—without me."

85

Larson's honest face flushed. "Yes," he declared. "I told the Committee that if yuh were informed of the meetin', I wouldn't attend. Yuh or me, I told 'em."

"So they took yuh—huh?" cried Wurt, stung despite himself. But he kept up the pretense of the offended citizen. "I'd like to know what yuh've got against me, Larson?"

"There's someone in the Gulch," cried Larson hotly, "who's behind every rotten thing that happens—"

"Meanin' me?" spat Wurt.

"Meanin' yuh!" yelled Larson, his wide mouth quivering.

"Maybe yuh got proof?" demanded Wurt, his voice falling low—and menacing.

"No, but I—" began Larson.

"Then yuh'd better keep yore trap shut!" snapped Wurt.

"Yuh're the one!" shouted Larson. "And by the great horn spoon, I'll get proof if it's the last thing I do."

"It will be the last thing yuh do," gritted Wurt. He strode to the door, jerked it open and slammed it violently shut.

13. The Hideout

THE MID-AFTERNOON SUN was settling westward when a much perturbed Ed Farrell kicked his burro out of Hangman's Gulch.

His leathery, weatherbeaten face, under his black, battered hat, was close-webbed with bewilderment, anxiety. It sat in his faded blue eyes and ran in a dejected line across his thin shoulders.

Ed Farrell, placer miner, was a simple man, who like thousands of others had followed the will-o'-the-wisp of the rich bar or rich diggings through the passes and gorges and ravines that honeycombed the gold fields. But unlike the others, he had finally struck it. Yet despite his good fortune, possession seemed to elude his grasp.

The oldster had no mind for the complexities of the

present situation. He was a man who always believed in the simplicity of black and white. But here he was suddenly confronted with other colors. Colors he could not recognize.

In a while, the wiry miner began to search the trail ahead of him with more than ordinary care. He knew by the clotted brush and tangle of distant trees he was nearing his claim.

"They ought to be 'round here," he muttered anxiously, "if they're goin' to be here-a-tall."

He slowed his pace. Then wide relief showed in his face, as the brush parted and Bide Evans and Ming Foy pushed to the trail.

"All set, Ed?" asked the lean, red-headed man.

Farrell shook his bandaged head despondently.

"What's wrong?" demanded Bide Evans. The oldster, he saw, wore a haggard, puzzled expression.

The gray-haired miner shook his head again. "Everythin'," he said. "Everythin'." He glanced despairingly at his partner.

"Talk is sometimes good," said Ming.

"The claims clerk says," declared Farrell, "that to transfer a claim in the Gulch, all parties got to be present."

"Why didn't yuh get my brother?" asked Bide. "He would have—"

"No," interrupted Farrell. "It wasn't that." It was painful for him to get it out. "The claim wasn't entered in yore brother's name."

"What!" cried Bide. Now he began to understand Matt's willingness to comply. If the claim was not recorded for Matt, then obviously any bill of sale Matt might give on it wasn't worth the paper written on. But—

"It was entered in yore name—Bide Evans." Farrell had said it finally, and he lifted a pair of questioning eyes to the Texan.

"My name!" For an instant, surprise flared through Bide Evans; and a graying grimness came to his eyes. "There's somethin' else, Ed." It was less a question than a hunch working him.

"Yeah." Almost reluctantly, Farrell pulled a white, folded paper from his pocket and handed it to Bide Evans.

The ghost of a smile touched Evans' face. Then, he gave the paper into the hands of Ming Foy.

The Chinaman's slant eyes were inscrutable as they scanned the sheet. Finally he handed it back.

"Ming Foy," he declared blandly, "cannot read English."

"Then I'll read it to yuh," said Bide. " 'Wanted for Murder,' " he read. " 'One thousand dollars reward, dead or alive—for Bide Evans.' " It was the identical poster he had shown Matt, except that his name had been substituted for his brother's. His glance swept the two partners.

The pig-tailed man from China spoke. "The price of every man," he said unblinkingly, "is set by himself. And it is written," he added, "that printers are lazy men and their mistakes are without number."

"Sure," cried Ed Farrell, certainty returning to his face. "It was a mistake."

The Texan felt a sudden warmth for these two men. "Ming's right, Ed," he declared. "I'll drop by at the printer's later—" He broke off abruptly, as he realized the problem confronting him. To protest the mistake would uncover Matt. But he was not ready for that yet.

Farrell thought he followed Bide. "That's the trouble," he said. "They got this Wanted poster plastered all over town. Someone's bound to see yuh and take a shot at yuh before the mistake's fixed."

Bide let it pass. "Looks like someone gave me a present of yore claim, Ed," he said. "But didn't intend me to give it back to yuh—or to get to use it myself. But we'll fool 'em." He smiled grimly.

"What are yuh goin' to do?" asked Ed, anxious-eyed.

"Since a transfer's no good in the Gulch without the parties appearin'," replied Bide, "I'll make yuh and Ming my heirs." Taking a pencil from his pocket, he wrote some words on the back of the Wanted poster. "So in case I die, yuh get the claim back in yore names. In the meantime, I'll add a note to this, sayin' yuh're workin' the claim for me. That's so no one can put yuh off."

Ed Farrell grinned. Things were back to black and white again. He accepted the paper from Bide.

"A clever man fools himself," said Ming Foy solemnly. "But an honest man fools no one—even himself."

"Let's go," said Bide, a smile gathering at the corners of his eyes, "and see them two gents who been workin' yore claim so hard all day—without pay."

The two partners laughed and Bide joined them. It was evident to the Texan that his two friends were not exactly clear on the business; but were willing to wait his explanation.

A stiff wind had come up and was working the trees. There was a hint of rain in it. The sun had already slid past the shoulder of the west. But it would not be dark for yet another half hour. In the meantime, Pete and Slim, the two hard, tough-looking men who had been working Farrell's claim, were knocking off for the day.

. Slim had a fire going by the time his companion had transferred the scrapings from the riffle cleats at the bottom of the rocker, to a milkpan.

They then heated the pan over the fire, and in a few minutes were able to blow away the hot sand. Dusk was fading into night as they stared, almost hypnotized, at the result of their day's diggings. The fire caught the feverish gleam in their eyes. Finally, the one named Pete spoke.

"Slim," he cried, and his voice was almost violent, "if this ain't the richest piece of pay dirt we worked yet, then I'm a Chinaman."

"Yuh're right, Pete," declared the other harshly. "Must be about two pounds in that pan." Avariciously he watched his friend pour the dull yellow flakes into a small bag. " 'Pears to me, Pete," he said suddenly, "that them's that work should get the benefits of their work."

"Huh?" Pete's mouth fell open. Then he understood. "Yeah," he cried. "Why should they get it—when we worked for it?"

"Yuh're right, friends. They shouldn't get it." A soft, mocking voice came floating to them across the clearing.

Like snarling, snapping wolves, Pete and Slim went hauling for their guns.

"Reach!" The voice suddenly crackled like a whiplash. "And don't go up limpin'!"

The two men were half-drawn when the owner of the voice slid into the clearing. He made a loose, tough shape against the semi-darkness and the Colt in his hand was infinitely menacing.

The gaunt man, Slim, decided to complete his draw. But it was a sad mistake. The gun in the newcomer's hand bucked and Slim's howl of pain rose and mingled with the shot's echo. Blood gushed from the nick in his hand. Without further delay, the two men complied with the stranger's request.

89

"All right, Ed," called Bide Evans, for it was he. "C'mon out, Ming."

The two partners came out of the shadows. Farrell carried his heavy rifle and a big six-shooter gaped incongruously from Ming's hand.

"Take the gold," directed Bide, "and throw their guns away."

"What's the big idea?" growled Pete. "Yuh damn claim-jumpers, we threw yuh out of here this mornin'."

Bide considered them briefly. "Didn't Matt tell yuh he sold the claim this mornin' to Ed Farrell?"

"Sold?" cried Slim. "He'd be a fool to— Say, who are yuh?"

"Matt's brother," said Bide. "Now get movin', yuh two," he ordered.

The Texan and his two friends took the angry, baffled men down to the stream and saw them ride off. Bide, watching, suddenly saw them stop in the distance and separate—one going into the brush, the other continuing. An idea seized him.

"Ed, Ming," he said quickly. "I want yuh to tail that *hombre* who went off the trail. I'll ride after the other. We'll meet here later."

Ed Farrell slapped his burro and started off. Ming Foy's pigtail piggled behind as he clung to his partner. The gray-haired miner had no difficulty in picking up the trail, for the man—he turned out to be the one called Pete—was making noise aplenty going through the brush scrub. Evidently Pete gave little thought to being followed, or was still angry enough at being deprived of the fruits of his labor, to care. In addition, a silvery moon showed fleetingly among dark, heavy masses and caught Pete's shadowy outline from time to time as he pushed his way through the night.

The wind was making a raw file on the treetops, whipping through the brush—so that the underfoot sounds made by the burro were lost in the scuffle. Minutes slipped by.

Ahead Pete suddenly plunged into a dark cluster of trees and vanished from sight. Farrell prodded the burro and soon entered the tree span. He pulled rein and listened intently. Just then, the moon slipped behind a large, black mass; abruptly all became darkness.

"Lost him," muttered Farrell.

"To stand still," said Ming from behind, "is to go nowhere."

"Yeah," muttered the oldster, "but where do yuh go in this danged dark?"

"Perhaps our patient friend beneath us," said Ming, "will show us the way."

Farrell shrugged his shoulders. "We can't be worse off." He lifted the reins and gave the burro its head.

The animal legged it ahead. For perhaps ten minutes it worked through the inky blackness, carrying its double load. Then it seemed to Farrell that the night became less durable. He strained his eyes, squinting.

Suddenly the moon sailed free and lighted the landscape with a hoary luminiscence.

"By the great horn spoon!" Farrell cried softly. "Look, Ming."

Their burro had led them to the entrance of a narrow, rocky defile. A giant fissure of nature had apparently occurred here. Enormous boulders dotted the steep sides of the gorge; and the two men started through it.

After a few hundred yards the gorge widened and spread flat into an almost oval-shaped pocket, covered with scrub and tangles and stubby pines.

It was eerily silent here. The wind was cut off by the palisades and each time the burro's iron-shod hoof struck a pebble, it clanged sharply in the night.

With startling clarity Farrell suddenly heard a horse neigh. He drew rein abruptly. The sound seemed amazingly close at hand. Quickly the oldster dismounted and leading the animal with Ming Foy still up, skirted the dense cottonwood clump diectly in front of them.

He completed a virtual half-circle of the clump, then hastily withdrew into the fringe. There, in the clear moonlight that filtered through the overhead divide stood a log-wood cabin. Lamplight streamed through the windows, and the rough jumble of man talk spread thinly across the clearing.

To the right of the building was a small horse corral. And the chuff and grind of horses putting their weight against the corral planks to scratch their hides sounded in the night.

"I'm goin' to have a look-see," said Farrell. "Yuh stay put, Ming."

Ming Foy demurred. He pointed out that as equal

partner, he was entitled to share the risks as well as the profits.

"Sure," whispered Farrell. "But this ain't a minin' prop-'sition. 'Sides, I'm older than yuh are and that kind of gives me the right to decide—don't it?"

Ming shook his head stubbornly. "My honorable friend and partner is too aged to take such risks. He should permit a man of younger years to assume the burden."

Farrell covered his mouth and guffawed: "Aged my tin dipper!" he cried. "Yuh told me only yesterday yuh're only a year younger'n me. Nothin' doin'. I'm goin'." He took the big Colt from Ming, shoved it into his trouser belt and clapped his partner affectionately on the knee. Then cautiously he angled off across the clearing and made it to a mesquite thicket halfway to the left of the cabin.

Stopping to recover his breath, the oldster gazed upward, past the overhanging cliffs. He grimaced. The moon was shining with a silvery brilliance that overlaid the clearing with a lucid, white light. But in another moment a black streamer enveloped the bright disc.

Considering this a happy omen, Farrell quit the mesquite and cat-footedly made the corner of the building. With his back to the wall, the aging placer miner edged along until he reached the shutterless window. Then removing his hat, he crouched and inched up to the sill.

It was a bare, one-room cabin, with a big round-top table and some chairs. At one end was a small stove and supply box.

There were six or seven men in the room—men with the stamp of the outlaw breed on them. Some were playing cards, others eased against the wall. Tobacco smoke drifted hazily about the one lamp hanging in the cabin's center.

Over in a corner, Farrell picked out the man he and Ming had trailed, Pete. The latter was talking and gesticulating to a huge, pock-marked fellow, whom Farrell suddenly recognized as Black Henry.

Black Henry's voice came through the window in loud, strident tones.

"That name 'Evans,'" he cried, "is beginnin' to rile me."

One of the card players at the table looked up. A knife had made a jagged scar from ear to mouth. Buck teeth sawed the air as he talked.

"Yuh said that last time, boss," he said. "When he done for, Lem?"

Black Henry wheeled on him. "Don't make no mistake about that *hombre*," he cried. "He's plenty tough."

"When are we movin' to town?" asked the buck-toothed card player. "I'm gettin' tired of this shack."

"Soon," declared Black Henry. "Maybe day or so. Wurt'll give us the word."

"Never savvied," muttered a Hound tilted against the wall, "how yuh ever took up with that two-bit saloon keeper, boss?"

"That two-bit gent's," said Black Henry softly, his glance swinging the room, "got more brains than all of yuh put together. 'Sides, the arrangement's been profitable—ain't it?"

"But we do all the work," protested Pete. "And he gets half the gold dust."

Black Henry looked thoughtful. "Maybe," he said. "Maybe."

"Understand," offered Pete, "the sheriff and his brother don't get on so good together. What's between 'em?"

Black Henry laughed raucously. "Just a killin'," he cried. "This jasper came lookin' for Matt with a Wanted poster in his pocket." He laughed again. "But when Wurt seen it, he snipped out the front name, had Matt print it up with his brother's name—and now it's Bide Evans that's a wanted man. Yuh seen the posters all over town this mornin'. Can't tell 'em apart."

"Never looked," said the scar-face Hound. "Figgered it might be me." Harsh laughter circled the room.

The blue eyes of Ed Farrell, peering over the window sill, blinked furiously. Here was the explanation for the poster. He cursed himself for having doubted the red-headed Texan.

14. Ming Foy

So INTENT was Farrell on the scene before him, that he failed to hear the soft-footed tread of booted feet. Not until they were directly behind him.

Then he whirled with agility amazing in a man of his age, and grabbed the big Colt from his trouser belt. But he was too late. Already a gun butt was descending on his head. By turning, he merely deflected the blow a trifle and was stunned instead of knocked out cold.

Dizzy, Farrell fought back weakly, trying to trigger his gun; but coarse, callous hands wrenched the weapon from him. Then he heard shouting and knew that men came rushing out of the cabin.

He was mauled and booted and could put up but little resistance. He felt his pockets being emptied and heard the yell go up when the gold bag was found. Then he was seized roughly, dragged into the cabin and thrown on a straight-backed chair under the lamp.

Slowly, as the scene crystalized before Farrell, he realized he was seated in a semi-circle, with himself as the focus, and slit-eyed men staring at him as the arc.

An explaining voice was speaking. "—so I left Ed at the entrance and I followed this jasper—" Moe Wilson squinted hard at the gray-haired miner. He sucked in his pinched cheeks. "—could of sworn he wasn't wearin' a black shirt." He shrugged his shoulders. "Well—I watched him leave his burro at the trees out there and creep up and listen. So I came up behind and knocked him. Good thing Wurt sent me after yuh."

"All right, Moe," grunted Black Henry. He turned to Pete, scowling. "He followed yuh here. The next time yuh get so danged careless—" Pete paled. "—there won't be a next time. Now get that burro into the corral." Without a word, Pete swung on his heels and went out.

Black Henry's eyes slanted to Farrell's face and sat there a moment. Then a coarse smile spread broad over his pock-marked face. "So Mr. Farrell got lonesome and decided to pay his amigo Black Henry a visit. And he brought his visitin' card—and his friend's picture." His eyes wandered to the little leather pouch on the table and the Wanted poster on which it sat; and then back again to Farrell. His expression changed. When his face lost its smile, it became ugly. He was no longer smiling. "Who're yuh playin' spy for, Farrell?" he rasped. "And how much did yuh hear? Don't figger on yore old pal, Bide Evans, to help yuh this time—'cause he ain't."

Farrell hid his drooping spirits behind a tough grin.

"Maybe not," he cried. "Maybe it'll be the Vigilantes this time."

The huge leader of the Hounds roared. "Tomorrer mornin' yuh start diggin' all over again! How much did yuh hear?"

"Enough to hang yuh!" snapped the oldster angrily. "All of yuh—yuh danged killers!" There was a deep contempt in him for the breed that Black Henry represented and it poured out in his voice. Moreover, inasmuch as his fate was settled, he felt that nothing he might say could affect a change for the worse. Besides, it made him feel better.

"Why yuh—" cried Black Henry, stepping in and swinging his huge hand. Farrell stiffened, waiting for the blow to fall. Somehow it didn't. The smile came suddenly again to the black-bearded leader's face. "Yuh're an old coot," said the latter, "and Black Henry was never one to go beatin' old men. 'Sides, yuh paid yore way in." He took the leather pouch from the table and dropped it into his pocket. Then he picked up the Wanted poster and read the writing on the back. He smiled crookedly.

"Mighty considerate of yore friend Bide Evans," he said, "to make yuh heir to yore own claim."

"That's a little more than yuh was willin' to do," cried Farrell grimly.

Black Henry's eyes glinted yellow in the light. "That's 'cause I'm a businessman," he said, his heavy lips lifting in a grimace. "And he ain't." Slowly, the big man tore the poster into small pieces and let them drift from his hand to the wooden floor. His smile was wider now. "There goes yore claim, Farrell."

"It was yuh," Farrell cried, "who stole the claim paper from Ming and entered it in Matt Evans' name. And then yuh switched it to Bide Evans. Wasn't it?" His blue eyes clung to the big man's face.

"Yeah," admitted Black Henry. "It won't make no dif-f'rence if yuh know that. Yuh ain't leavin' the gorge. 'Sides, yuh're the only one who ever saw me at work. Can't afford to have yuh breathin'."

Farrell said, "They said yuh're playin' the smartest claim-jumpin' game in the whole gold fields."

Faint amusement and pride sat on Black Henry's thick lips as they pulled back in a smile. "So far," he admitted modestly.

"How does this Wurt *hombre* fit in?" asked Farrell.

Black Henry considered him carefully. Then he shook his head and sniggered in his beard. "Maybe I better not tell yuh, Farrell," he said. "Got to keep the game clean of competitors." He roared and his men roared with him.

Pete came back. Farrell could not refrain from heaving a sigh of relief, for the tough, stubbled gang member came alone. But his relief was short-lived.

Black Henry was watching his face through shrewdly narrowing eyes. "Where's yore pardner—that Chinaman?" he snapped suddenly.

Farrell showed him a bland, unblinking front. "Ming?" he said evenly. "Left him at the diggin's."

The huge leader's fox-eyes lifted and swung to the pinched, scarred face of Moe Wilson. "Moe," he said quickly, "what was the color of the shirt yuh thought Farrell was wearin'?"

Moe Wilson screwed his eyes up. "Huh?" he said. "Oh —I thought it looked kind of red like."

"Red?" cried Black Henry, turning back to the oldster. "Maybe the color was orange—huh, Farrell? Left him at the diggin's, huh? Yuh danged liar!"

"No I ain't," cried Farrell, with a sinking feeling, knowing suddenly what was coming next.

Oddly, Black Henry wasn't angry. As a matter of fact he seemed pleased with his deductions. He turned to face his men.

"That Chinaman's in our gorge, boys," he cried. "Go out there and find him. He can't get out, Ed's at the entrance. But we can't have him runnin' loose in here— even if he is harmless. I'll wait till yuh grab him." As the men started through the door, guns drawn, he called back two of them. "Pete, Wilson—tie up this old coot."

In a few moments, the gray-haired placer miner was neatly trussed, arms tied behind his back and bound to the chair legs. Black Henry looked on with amused interest. But eyes, other than the latter's were watching Farrell made helpless. The slanting eyes of Ming Foy.

Ming Foy was an obstinate man with cautious habits. But underneath the black mandarin hat he wore, was an agile, quick brain.

He had attended, in his youth, the University of China, and on the news of the gold strike, had with much trepidation, embarked for the new world. He had moderate ambitions and wanted no more than enough gold to bring his wife and seven children to California, and to be able to support them without fear of the morrow. He had seen the possibility of the fruition of his ambition, when he and his partner had struck paydirt at Dutch Diggings. Then had begun the series of events which had taxed his patience and goodwill—and led him to where he was at this moment—looking on while his partner and friend was being tied hand and foot. The last event happened thus:

He had been watching Farrell's actions for a few moments. The latter was no sooner at the cabin window when he heard a faint crunching sound to his left rear. Sliding off the burro, Ming stepped back further into the shadows.

Just then, a man, gun in hand, passed by the tree fringe, so close that Ming might have touched him with his rifle. There was no doubt in his mind that this man boded no good for his partner. But Ming Foy was not a fighting man—nor were the instincts of a fighting man his.

Otherwise, he might have leaned out and tapped the newcomer on the head with the heavy wooden stock of the rifle, and thus ended abruptly the danger to his partner. But he didn't think of it until the man had passed—and then it was too late.

He watched the man cautiously follow in Farrell's footsteps. He was tempted to call out several times, just as he was tempted to follow this newcomer. But he did nothing, for he knew the slightest noise would bring the men inside the cabin tumbling out. Moreover, Ming Foy had cautious habits, and was chained by them. But only for a while.

He started forward as soon as he saw the man with the gun move up on his partner. He was at the mesquite bush when the fight occurred and the men came shouting out to subdue Ed Farrell. Ruefully he measured his chances in the fray—and decided they weren't good.

Then when the clearing became deserted and quiet, he made the side of the cabin and leaned against the wall next to the window. Nothing said inside escaped his ears, for the window was open and Ming Foy attentive.

He smiled faintly when Pete went for the burro and realized how his partner must have felt. But his smile departed when he heard that the entrance and exit to the gorge was blocked. That meant that even if he could get

97

his partner released, they wouldn't be able to leave this place. Then, when Black Henry deduced that he, Ming, was in the pocket, and sent his men out to search for him, he knew it would not be long before he was found.

Ming Foy was definitely not a man of action. But he realized that the time had come for him to act. Even so he hesitated, but again recognizing the necessity, he squared his shoulders, put the rifle down, walked to the cabin door—and gave himself up.

Ed Farrell, seated facing the door, got the surprise of his life when Ming Foy walked in alone. His eyes widened, his chin dropped; a queer disbelieving look came to his face. Black and white were the only colors the aging placer miner could see; and this didn't look white.

"How are you, gentlemen?" Ming Foy said blandly. And he smiled a wide, foolish smile.

"Well I'll be—" cried Black Henry. "Here he is!" He drew for his gun, but halfway through decided against it and let the weapon slide back into holster. "Search him, Pete. Moe, call the boys back."

Pete handled Ming Foy roughly. "Nope," he told his chief, and pushed the Chinaman into a chair next to his partner. Outside, Moe Wilson could be heard yelling; and soon the men came drifting back.

When they were all returned, Black Henry said, "He's harmless, boys. Gave himself up. Just keep him tied. I'll be back tomorrer mornin'. C'mon, Wilson, and yuh three; we'll pick Ed up on the way."

Farrell heard the sounds of horses moving off in the night and then fade away in the distance. A card game started between Pete and a second outlaw named Lippy, wide-lipped, squat; and the scar-cheeked member of the gang stood before Ming Foy and gave his consideration.

"Well, Chinee?" demanded this one, as he started coiling a rawhide around Ming Foy's limbs. "How do yuh like this country?"

"How are you, gentlemen?" said Ming Foy blandly. "Me belly hungry," and he patted his belly.

The buck-toothed outlaw gaffawed and turned to Farrell. "What kind of a pardner did yuh pick yoreself, miner?"

A puzzled frown sat on Ed Farrell's brow. "Don't know," he answered. "Don't know."

"Me belly hungry," repeated Ming Foy. "Me fine cook."

The two men playing cards looked up suddenly. "Cook!" cried Pete. "Why the heck didn't he say so? Bill," he cried to the buck-toothed outlaw, "lay off that. Our problem's settled; we just got ourselves a cook."

Ed Farrell's eyes twinkled. The color was white again. His partner had something up his sleeve.

"The boss said to tie him," objected Bill.

"Yeah," cried Pete. "But he didn't know he could cook. 'Sides, Black Henry said he was harmless."

That settled it. In a moment, the coils fell away from Ming Foy and soon he had a dinner sizzling on the fire that kept the outlaws' heads turning continually toward the stove.

Ming's first meal was a great success and he was permitted to partake of it and to feed his partner.

Afterward, the card game broke up. Outside it started to rain. Ming Foy was bound and placed on the dirty brown blanket on the floor next to Ed Farrell. Soon the lamplight was blown out and the chatter of the outlaws' talk dwindled away. Only the sound of the rain that found its way past the narrow overhead gap, was heard on the cabin roof.

Much later, when steady snoring made the cabin sound like a hornet's nest, Ed Farrell felt pressure against him. Then he heard Ming's soft voice at his ear.

"Will bring help in morning," breathed the Chinaman, "if I can get away."

Morning broke bright and clear. The cabin woke up slowly. Then Ming Foy was roused and let loose to prepare breakfast.

Ming worked a while at the stove then turned to Pete who was keeping an eye on him. "Need water," he said.

"C'mon outside," said Pete. "Show yuh where it is."

Ed Farrell watched them go out and thought he caught a steely glint from his partner's black eyes. Minutes passed.

Bill finally got restless. "Say what happened to 'em?" He rose and went to the door. Suddenly, Farrell saw him dive back into the room for his gun belt, seize his guns and let loose at the doorway. Then the gray-haired miner heard the thud of driving hoofs, pounding the turf hard.

The two outlaws went flying out of the cabin. Anxiously,

Farrell waited. In a few moments, Pete came in, holding his head. He was complaining to Bill:

"—damned Chinee hit me on the head with the bucket —and I went out like a light."

"Harmless—huh?" cried Bill, looking over to Farrell. "All right, mister," he told the miner grimly. " 'Stead of breakfast—yuh're goin' to start diggin'. Now!"

15. Murder

BACK AT DUTCH DIGGINGS Bide Evans pulled his black out of the brush and swung into leather. The claim-jumper ahead of him was fading into the moonlit distance. Bide let his mount out and soon the other hove in sight. It was the one called Slim. The man's bandaged hand made a white blob against his horse's dark skin.

Slim kept a warm jog along the stream. After a while, Bide realized the man he followed was heading for Hangman's Gulch. It no longer mattered then, when the moon slid out of sight. He merely held to the stream and listened to the steady thud of hoofs ahead. The wind that had sprung up moist to his face, blew from the west and brought the clip-clop of Slim's horse clearly to him.

Once the wind veered and Bide reined up abruptly, aware that the horse sounds had sudenly ceased. Then after a moment the wind beat back, and up ahead hoofs began to fall again. Evidently Slim had thought he heard something, then decided he had been mistaken. Nonetheless, the Texan proceeded with greater caution and stayed further behind, keeping to the shadows when the bright moon was in the clear.

"Maybe I shouldn't have sent 'em," he worried half-aloud, his face troubled with a frown.

He had begun to feel sorry that he had set the partners on the trail of the other claim-jumper. There was a definite risk of danger for Farrell and Ming. Moreover, what he expected to learn was yet hardly clear in his own mind. Perhaps that was why he had to collect all the information he could.

He realized that unwittingly he had become involved in an odd and highly dangerous situation. He had entered the Gulch with a single, simple purpose—that of taking his brother back to Dudley, Texas, for the murder of old Abe Symes. And overnight he had become the hunted instead of the hunter.

The Vigilantes had become acutely suspicious of him; his brother's unsavory reputation had fallen on him; the murder charge had been switched to him; and Matt had become sheriff—all in all, a ticklish situation.

Yet more and more he was coming to feel that Matt had been framed. This despite the trick that Matt had played on him with the Wanted poster. Ruefully, he realized that the Gulch now regarded him as a desperado. He thought of Kate Larson and wondered about her.

Abruptly he rememberd something that had slipped from Wurt: that it would be awkward for him if Matt were elected. Well, Matt was sheriff—and it was awkward. A connection? Bide shrugged his shoulders. Perhaps.

Fragmentary incidents passed fleetingly through his brain: the three men from Wurt's saloon; Matt and Wurt waving Black Henry and his men after him—then he had assumed it was Matt—perhaps it had been Wurt; and the fear in Wurt's face at their first meeting.

His mind stopped short on that. Fear! That was the key to Wurt. Wurt feared him. Why? Before Bide could turn this over in his mind, he saw Slim's gaunt figure suddenly etched against the lights of Hangman's Gulch.

Bide Evans hitched his black under a wide oak at the outskirts and came in afoot. It began to rain as he entered town—a light, misty drizzle. Pulling his wide-brimmed hat well down, he hastened up the street. He smiled grimly as he passed fresh posters tacked on walls, with his brother's picture, but bearing his name.

The drizzle had cut the street crowd and his long stride took him quickly toward the Star saloon, where he had seen Slim dip off his mount and enter.

In a few moments, Bide shouldered past a group of greasy-faced, drunken miners and quietly pushed past the batwings. He blinked in the yellow glare of the overhead lamps and flash of the back bar mirror, and moved aside to the wall. A kind of Babel filled the room, with drinking, swearing miners shouting at each other to make themselves heard over an increasing din.

In the brief glance he cast over the saloon, Bide noticed that the Star had a second floor with an open balustrade showing several doors. There was a stairway leading up there at the right end of the bar. Eyes narrowed, he searched the haze and smoke lifting to the lamps—and found Slim at the bar.

The latter had just downed a drink, weaved through the crowd and went through that door.

Swiftly, Bide wheeled out of the saloon. Stepping off the porch to the right, he went into the alley and cut through its darkness. The room Slim had gone into was at the opposite side of the saloon; he therefore had to circle the building.

Quickly, he made the end corner, and noticed the sloping shed that ran off the second floor. He filed that away in his mind. Silently he turned the second corner and footed it forward, now in the direction of the street. As he ran, he felt the cool drizzle trickle down his neck.

He slowed, feeling that there ought to be a door near. Still moving forward, he groped along the wall. Suddenly, a form, darker than the blackness, came lurching out toward him, almost knocking him down.

A gasp of surprise was wrenched from this other man. Reaching out to keep from falling, Bide threw his hands out instinctively and caught on to the other's coat. There was a ripping sound and Bide felt the coat give way. It was wet to the touch. A muffled oath escaped the man's lips and he lashed out.

Bide felt it coming and threw his fist. As his knuckles scraped against his opponent's jaw, his boots slipped in the alley mud, made soggy by the rain, and he went down.

He was up in an instant, but only just in time to hear a door clicking shut. Then, realizing that the alley wasn't going to be a safe spot in the next few minutes, Bide retraced his steps on the run, circled the building—and then after brushing off his clothes, sauntered onto the porch again.

He placed his shoulder against the shadowed wall under the front shed and tapered up a smoke. He had thrown a scare into someone, and wondered idly who it was.

He sent out a ring of smoke into the cool night air, and noticed that the main street had grown much darker. The rain had put the flares out. Three or four riders whirled out of the increasing gloom of the town. They came up to the Star in a flurry, threw their reins over the hitch rail and stomped into the saloon. A whisper ran across the porch, "Black Henry."

Bide took a long drag on his cigarette, slowly exhaled the whitish smoke and then flipped it into the middle of the street. He watched it cut a glowing arc through the night and sizzle out as it hit wet dirt. Then he pushed out from the wall, felt at his Colts and once again entered the Star.

Hunching slightly, he sidled along the edge of the room, making his way toward the table at which sat the huge, black-bearded man and his followers. They were passing a bottle around, laughing roughly. One of the men rose and Bide heard Black Henry's deep-chested voice:

"Tell him to come down here, Moe. I'm gettin' tired of candles. 'Sides, ain't he a good friend of the sheriff's?"

Bide edged into a chair, tipped it back against the wall and pushed his hat down over his face. He had seen the man named Wilson start up the stairs to the second floor. He waited, listening. Suddenly he stiffened. Black Henry was talking.

"Yuh two," he was saying, "will work Farrell's claim startin' tomorrer mornin'; it's a good one." He chuckled in his beard. "Farrell and that Chinaman are goin' to be too busy at the cabin to pay it any attention from now on."

Shadows flurried darkly around Bide's deep-set eyes, and his lips became one thin, tight line.

"Shouldn't have sent 'em," bitterly escaped him.

He shifted his hat slightly and saw Jim Wurt coming down the stairs with the man named Wilson behind. Wurt was a well-groomed man, he had to admit; long frock coat, carefully brushed hair, freshly shaven. Then the latter was at Black Henry's table.

Bide's hat came down again and if anyone had looked his way, they would have seen what appeared to be a drunken cowboy.

"We agreed to meet in the back room," Wurt said in a curt voice.

"Too dark for me," grunted Black Henry. "I like the light and noise. Anyhow, it's time."

"Yeah," agreed Wurt finally. "It's time." Evidently Wilson had told Wurt of Farrell and Ming, for his next

103

words were: "Understand yuh want to cash some gold dust, tonight?"

"That's right," cried Black Henry, laughing hintingly. He thumped his pocket. "Dutch Diggin's gold—the best there is."

"Then come into my office," said Wurt, rising. "I'll weigh it for yuh."

Black Henry got to his feet and pushed the chair back, when a voice with a by-now familiar drawl, drifted past his ear.

"Just a second, gents."

The thick-chested man whirled fast, hand shooting for holster. Six inches from gun butt, it froze, as if meeting a stone wall. Staring at him was the black, gaping end of a big Colt. His men behind him stared and froze with him.

Bide made a rough, crankling shape back against the wall, his grim smile definitely tough, his Colt a violent, hawking menace.

"I'll take that gold, Mr. Henry," he said softly.

"It's Bide Evans!" Wurt cried, his lips drawn in a sudden snarl. "Don't give it to him."

"Shut up, Wurt!" snapped Bide, his attention on the big man. The latter stood silent, his fox-eyes fixed carefully on him, watching—waiting for the attention of the crowd to pull this way. Bide put his hand out. "The bag, *hombre*. Don't forget, the claim at Dutch Diggin's is in my name."

A slow smile rolled over Black Henry's pocked face. His big teeth showed white. "Yeah," he growled. "It is yores." Slowly he pulled the bag from his pocket. Then he began to laugh and his huge body shook with mirth. "Yeah," he agreed, tears rolling down his eyes, "the joke is on us." He threw the leather bag.

Bide went there, picked the cuffs up and pulled a "Thanks," he said. Through the corner of his eyes, he saw that the crowd was watching him now. He could feel the tension mount. A heavy, oppressive silence began to weigh against him. He pulled his other Colt and backed to the door. Black Henry grinned and put pressure on him.

"What's yore hurry, friend? Stay and have a drink."

Bide's mouth was dry at the roof. But he grinned back, a hard, hot grin. Then, a break came, but from an unexpected source. The batwings were suddenly flung open and a man came in on the run, his face red with excitement.

"Hey, Wurt," he called, not seeing Bide for the moment. "Larson's been found shot. Murdered—" His voice petered out suddenly.

But the Texan was already taking advantage of the interruption. As the newcomer pulled at the strings of the crowd's attention, he hipped around and bolted the saloon.

Hubbub rose shrill after him. Wurt's voice sounded high, frantic. "Get him!" the latter cried fiercely. "There's a thousand dollars on his head. I'll add another to it. Get the killer!"

Holstering his Colts, Bide legged it across the street on a diagonal run. Shots came roaring, nipping after him as he made the corner of the building and hugged the alleyside to catch his breath. Wood splinters ricocheted past his face and the sound of yelling men came close.

"So he'll add a thousand to it," he muttered. Then, "I better get moving if I don't want the whole Gulch down on my neck."

He plunged into the darkness of the alley. He pulled up abruptly at its end, almost plunging into the stream. He cut left and sped toward the west end of the town, following the course of the waterway. Sounds behind him trailed off.

"Shook 'em," he muttered, panting. Then, "This ought to take me to the hoosegow."

It did. In a short while, he pulled up behind the town jail. He snaked around the far side, as he had done that morning and quietly made his way to the front. A yellow shaft of light came from the office window; and with it the murmur of two or three voices.

As Bide paused at the edge of the jail, the door suddenly opened and two shadows were cast into the yard. An unfamiliar voice sounded.

"Three hours of poker with yuh, Matt, is aplenty for me."

"Me, too," a second voice added.

Bide heard Matt's voice now. " 'Night, Clark. 'Night, Smith. Yuh got to come from Texas to have the savvy."

" 'Night," the two called. The light from the door faded and Bide heard the two men mount up and jog off. Then

105

he came around the front, and without hesitation, opened the door and walked in.

Matt had just taken his gun belt off and hung it on the wall. He flushed and made a motion for it when he saw his visitor.

"Don't trouble, Matt," said Bide, wiggling his drawn gun.

"Yuh again?" muttered Matt sullenly.

"Yeah," said Bide, his eyes touching his brother's face. Something odd stirred in him. "I'm in a hurry, Matt. Give me the badge."

Wordlessly, scowling, the latter took off the star and handed it to him. Bide glanced briefly around the room, searching. Then he found what he wanted. A pair of steel handcuffs were lying on the desk. The keys lay next to them.

Bide went there, picked the cuffs up and pulled a chair over the grilled window. Snapping one steel cuff shut around one of the window bars, he motioned Matt to sit down.

"What's the idea?" growled Matt; but he complied.

Bide clicked the second steel cuff on Matt's wrist. "Want to keep yuh here till I get back," he said. "Larson was just murdered—know anythin' about it?"

Matt said, "No."

Bide considered him. "If yuh give me yore word yuh won't yell," he said. "I won't have to gag yuh."

Matt sneered. "What's my word worth to yuh?"

"Whatever yuh say it is, Matt," Bide said evenly.

Matt flushed. "All right," he said after a moment.

Bide thumbed his finger at the bulletin board. "Yore idea, Matt?"

Matt looked at the Wanted poster, and suddenly grinned. "Looks like yuh—huh?"

Bide said, "Don't think it's funny."

Matt said, "I do."

Bide smiled thinly, again noting the likeness between his brother and himself. He blew out the lamp and went to the door. He turned. "Where did yuh say yuh lost yore gold charm, Matt?"

"Thought I lost it at Jim's—" began Matt. He halted abruptly. "What diff'rence does it make to yuh?"

"Some," said Bide. "Where did Jim get the money to buy a saloon?"

"Poker," grunted Matt.

"See yuh later," Bide said, and went out.

16. Sheriff Evans Takes Over

"HOWDY, SHERIFF," someone called, and Bide Evans
nodded.

The crowd in front of Sam Larson's general store made
way for the man with the tin star pinned to his vest. There
was a jam in the store also and Bide had to shoulder
his way through. When he got to the counter over which
the one lamp in the place shed a yellow glow, he turned.

"All right," he said. "Clear out."

Slowly, the crowd thinned, and in a few moments
only a small group remained in the corner, near the
railed-off desk with the scale and weights on it.

Bide went over to them, his eyes sizing the scene. A
blanketed figure lay stretched at the rail, and a thin, red
trickle of blood showed from one end of the blanket. Kate
Larson was there, a strain pulling white at her face and
making her eyes wide, tragic. Judge Carter was there, his
goatee a silvery triangle in the half shadows. Tay Brown
was there, dark-faced, grim; Dan Rivers, hard-mouthed;
others.

Behind the desk, he noted, the large safe doors were
open. They showed him a wide hostility as he came up.
A curious resolve came suddenly to Bide Evans. His brother had a bad name. Perhaps—

"Sorry, Miss Larson," Bide said. To Rivers: "Who
found him?"

"Yuh're not wanted here, Evans," said Brown curtly.
"We'll find the ornery killer ourselves!"

Bide's eyes rested on Brown's face, cool, deliberate.
"I'm lawman in the Gulch, Brown," he said quietly.
"When I want yore help I'll ask for it."

"Why yuh—" cried Brown, flushing.

Bide's elbows hooked back fast—then relaxed. "I
wouldn't start any trouble, Brown," he said, cold steel
in his voice. "I came in to learn what happened."

107

Unexpectedly Judge Carter spoke: "He's in the right, Brown. He's the legal arm of the law in Hangman's Gulch. We'll just have to—er, put up with him."

Bide drawled, "Thanks, Judge." A thin smile edged off his lips. "Now—who found Larson?" Just then the store door opened and Jim Wurt strode in. He doffed his hat and came immediately to the girl. His black mustache caught a glint from the lamp.

"I just heard," Wurt told her. "I'm terribly sorry, Kate." Then he said, nodding, "Howdy, Sheriff—hello, men."

Bide's eyes widened imperceptibly and they rode back from Wurt's face to Kate Larson's. He read nothing in the latter—perhaps a faint tinge of annoyance. But Wurt's face had flushed faintly as his eyes rested on the girl.

That told Bide something; and as his gaze went to the others, their reserve toward the newcomer told him something again. Then hulking, flabby Dan Rivers spoke up, answering the question he had asked.

"I found Sam, Sheriff," Rivers said. "Came in for some tobacco 'bout half an hour ago— He was layin' there with two bullets in him—the safe cleaned out."

A certain coincidence leaped at Bide and hit him between the eyes.

"I had just left my father," Kate Larson added, her voice flat, her eyes cold. "He was closing up for the night— putting away all the miner's gold-dust bags for safe-keeping—"

Judge Carter patted her on the shoulder. "Maybe you'd better get home, Kate," he advised. "Brown, will you—?"

"No," declared Kate. "I'll stay." Bide felt her eyes on him, chill, unfriendly. "Rivers," she said slowly, "says he saw a redheaded man go through the back door, just as he came in."

Wrinkles ran webs circling Bide's eyes as they narrowed to thin, gray slits. Abruptly, he grabbed off his wide-brim and stepped back under the lamp. "This color, Rivers?" he snapped.

A damp, trickly silence clamped down on the store. A rat, scampering behind the counter, made fast, clicking sounds as it ran. Then the faint echo faded away.

Dan Rivers moved his bulk slowly to the light, his baggy, ink-stained trousers making him shapeless from the hips down. He blinked owlishly.

108

"Looks like," he muttered finally. He took his pencil out and fooled with it.

"Listen to me—all of yuh," cried Bide, his voice driving out at them. "I know none of yuh trust me, and maybe yuh have reason for it. But I had nothin' to do with this —and I'd like to see the killer hung as much as any of yuh!" Later, when he thought of it, he realized it was neither he nor Matt speaking, but an Evans. Family pride, they called it.

For a second, his voice held them. Then Tay Brown broke through with a contemptuous sneer. "Sam always said yuh were a good speechmaker, Evans," he declared.

Hot words leaped to Bide's lips, then he caught Kate's eyes on him. There was a strange change in their hazel depths and they regarded him queerly—almost curiously. Quickly he replaced his hat, remembering she knew he had gray eyes, Matt green. He wondered if she had noticed the scar on his neck, and moved away from the light.

"Clark and Smith," he said evenly, "have been playin' cards with me for the last three hours. Is that good enough, Judge?"

"After we checked on it," snapped Tay Brown.

Jim Wurt's voice sounded, unanticipated, from the semi-shadows near the railing. It was empty of expression.

"I think we can believe the sheriff," he said.

"Why?" demanded Brown brusquely.

"Because I saw the party that did the killin'," replied Wurt evenly.

A second's surprise held them.

Bide said, "Suppose yuh tell what and who yuh saw, Mr. Wurt." A premonition rankled through him as he caught the glitter in Wurt's black eyes.

"Sure, Sheriff," said Wurt. There was an obvious deference and respect in his voice when he addressed the Gulch's lawman. "I was standin' on the porch of the Star, 'cross the street, 'bout half an hour ago and was just goin' in, when I see someone come runnin' out of the alley along here—" He paused, then continued:

"Then this gent cuts across the street to where his black horse is hitched. I got a good look at his face when he went up into saddle. Then he lit out—out of town."

"And who was this gent, Wurt?" asked Bide softly, knowing the answer in advance.

"Yore brother, Sheriff," said Wurt. "Bide Evans."

109

A tight-drawn gasp was touched off. Bide's eyes, slanting over, caught Kate's hand at her face, her lips pressed tight.

"So it was that killer?" cried the gambler.

Bide said, "Sure it was my brother, Wurt?"

"I didn't like to say it, Sheriff," said Wurt earnestly, " 'cause I don't exactly know how yuh feel about him. But I'd swear it was Bide Evans on a stack of Bibles."

"Heard a Chinaman once say," declared Bide softly, "that if yuh pile them Bibles too high, they're likely to fall."

Jim Wurt took a step forward. The light touched his face—showed it grow sallow, dark.

"What do you mean by that, Evans?" he demanded angrily.

Bide closely watched the puzzled light dance in the opaque depths of Wurt's eyes. About to speak, Bide was cut off by the girl. Surprisingly, she asked the question he was going to put.

"How can you tell the difference between the sheriff and his brother?" she demanded. "They look alike. I've seen them both."

Something else came into Wurt's eyes, Bide saw. The spectre of fear. Then it vanished. But Wurt's answer was right and held no hint of that fear. Again Bide paid out an unwilling admiration for this small man's nimble, swift-thinking mind. Despite the fact that the story Wurt told was a lie from beginning to end.

"Clark and Smith," said Wurt, "came into my place five minutes ago for a drink. They told me they had just spent a few hours with the sheriff."

"It was Bide Evans, all right," cried Tay Brown. His poster's all over town. He's wanted in Texas for murder."

"Looks like," Bide said evenly, "the Evans family's gettin' itself a bad name in Hangman's Gulch."

"You earned it!" cried Kate Larson angrily, flushing.

"I ain't so sure," said Bide slowly, his face building up hard. "In Texas we had a good name."

"That's right," put in Judge Carter surprisingly. "I stopped by at the Evans ranch several years ago. You were away, Sheriff—and so was your brother. But Luke Evans, your father, has one of the best names in Texas."

"Thanks, Judge," said Bide. "But before we jump to

conclusions and accuse my brother of murder, let's make sure he did it."

The printer's voice floated in the room. "Yuh mean Wurt was seein' things, Sheriff?"

Bide's eyes shifted from face to face. Wurt was puzzled, angry—uncertain. Kate Larson's eyes were uncomfortably steady on his face. Judge Carter was watching him thoughtfully. Tay Brown had lost his aggressive assurance. They all had the look as if something had come into the room—something new and disturbing.

"I ain't sayin' anythin'," Bide declared, "until I've looked into it. First place, Wurt didn't see my brother come out of the store—he came out of the alley. Second place, all Rivers seen was red hair. Big town like the Gulch can have more than two heads of red hair—huh? Third place, Bide ain't a killer."

"Ain't he wanted in Texas?" demanded Brown.

Bide said: "Mistake," and let it go at that. He had the makings out and was tapering up a smoke. But his eyes were on Wurt. The latter had been listening to him with a peculiar intentness. Blood came and went across the saloon owner's face, leaving it ghastly one minute, red the next. *He suspects,* Bide thought.

He turned to the girl, aware that her eyes hadn't left his face. "Miss Larson," he asked, "did yore father have any enemies? Did he quarrel with anyone lately?" Again he felt something respond inside him as he looked at her.

"Yes," she said evenly. "He quarreled with your— brother. And with Mr. Wurt."

"Ah," he said. It was evident from the glances directed at Wurt and then at Kate, that the others knew of the quarrel between Wurt and Larson and were aware of its reason. Then he too suddenly divined its origin. Unaccountably it made him feel better. "Mr. Wurt," he said casually, "I reckon yuh can tell us where yuh were half hour ago?"

It was actually an idle question, but for a moment, he thought something cracked inside the blank mirror of Wurt's eyes. But the latter's voice was entirely unruffled.

"Of course I can," said Wurt quietly. "If necessary."

"Where?" asked Bide, gently insisting.

Wurt flushed. "I don't see any reason for it," he said half-angrily. "But I was in my saloon."

"Good enough," said Bide. "I'm goin' to have a look-see

around." He moved toward the side door, through which the murderer had left, according to Rivers. He smiled thinly as he went into the next room. He knew he had done two things in there. He had made them uncertain that the evidence was sure proof of Bide Evans' guilt; and he had begun to destroy the picture they had in their minds of Matt Evans.

He left the door open and the light that ran along the store's counter drifted in here, and showed it to be a small room, used for an office and for storing excess merchandise. Flour and coffee bags were piled against the walls. There was a desk and chair in the corner.

There was another door at the opposite end. He crossed over and pushed it open. The sound of the rushing stream smote his ears. Water flowed directly behind the building; there was no more than a ridge of three or four feet between the stream and store. In the dark he could make out the white froth eddies formed by rocks at the edge of the bank.

If anyone came out of here on the run, he reflected, they couldn't help but hit the stream. Recent memory cut across his thoughts like a whip. That man he had run into in the Star alley had been wet. The coat he had grasped and torn had been wet. And the man had vanished into Wurt's saloon!

The pressure of the thought eased off. It was drizzling then and he recalled the feel of the rain on the back of his neck. Yet the thought persisted that the man's coat had been *very* wet. He shrugged his shoulders and went back into the store.

The store was empty now, save for the water-eyed, bony undertaker, Dud Harvey, and a helper. Apparently they had just entered; and were making their lugubrious preparations. Dud Harvey looked up and his sad face became sadder.

"Howdy, Sheriff," he said hesitatingly.

"What kind of a gun—?" asked Bide. And he nodded toward the figure lying under the blanket.

"Derringer, looks like," replied Harvey, and turned back to his work.

The *juzgado* lay dark and silent when Bide approached it. There was nothing about it to indicate a change had taken place. Yet subtle indications of danger reached out to him and slowed his pace.

112

His hands were on his pistol butts when he pushed the door open with his boot. Nothing stirred in there.

"Matt," he called.

"Yeah?" It was Matt's voice from the window.

Then Bide saw his brother's blurred outline in the dark and stepped into the room. Something moved behind him. He twirled— His instincts had been right, but he had not listened carefully. The point of a pistol ground into his spine, and he brought up stock still as a voice cracked in his ear:

"Freeze!"

A light went on. Wurt stood there, his eyes full of hatred, a hectic flush on his face. Matt sat at the window, but the steel handcuffs were off his wrists. And a mocking smile rode his face as he came up, took the badge from Bide's vest and the guns from his holsters.

Two other men were there. One Bide recognized as the man called Wilson; the other was his old friend, Slim, who leered at him as he held a gun against his back.

"A smart gent that likes to play games—huh," cried Wurt. "Yuh're goin' to stretch for that killin' tonight, Bide Evans."

Bide saw Matt's eyebrows lift. "He done in Larson?" the latter asked Wurt.

"Yeah!" cried Wurt sharply.

Bide said, "The killer made a mistake, Matt—just like he did in Dudley. He used a derringer tonight. That other night, he planted a gold charm in the paralyzed right hand of a left-handed man."

17. Turned Tables

BIDE EVANS stirred restlessly on the wooden plank bunk. Finally, finding sleep impossible, he got up and took to pacing the small, stuffy cell. But he found no outlet across the short floor for the muscles that craved action, for the crowded feeling that cried out for release. A foreboding stirred in him like the first faint ruffling of a wind-boding storm.

He stopped at the cross-bar window and looked out into the night. It lay dark and heavy—and without rain now. He saw nothing; heard only the rush of the stream. The moon remained hidden behind scabrous, dingy masses and the cool breeze had been stifled into close, choking air.

He wheeled away from the window and fell to pacing again. Angrily, like a man who had made a mistake. A latent temper that matched the color of his hair was seeking a focus.

He forced his teeth into his lips and felt the bite of pain. It eased him somewhat. He faced his mistake squarely. He had been proud and had let Wurt find him out. He should have known Wurt would be at the jail waiting for him.

The thought of Farrell and Ming quickened his sense of frustration. He had sent them on an errand; and now he had failed them. He set down Matt as a personal failure too. Again it was his pride and stubborn sense of right and wrong that had stopped him from treating Matt as a brother. That's why, he felt, Matt had stood by tonight and let Wurt run things—let Wurt lock him up in this cell. The thought rankled.

Something stirred in the night and he was at the window again. He strained his eyes, listening intently, yet nothing touched his senses. But the cold chill that crawled down his spine kept giving him messages.

Out there, half-strangulated echoes whimpered through an implacable gloom. He felt the stifling, breathless night coil like a tightening noose around his neck. Blurred darkness swelled, expanded, contracted. The night held a deadly menace that hovered like the bird of death, ready to feed on carrion.

A pale shaft of light swinging suddenly down the dusty jail corridor, brought Bide Evans around, rigid. A lantern, dangling from a man's bandaged hand, approached his cell. Reaching the grilled door, it lifted, revealing the face of its carrier—Slim, gaunt, ugly-eyed.

Slim tilted the lantern against the bars and sent his eyes peering after the small light into the cell. He saw Bide leaning against the wall.

"Yuh're up," he said. Unease shifted through his eyes like a shadow.

Bide waited, the muffled sounds of the night a shrill

warning in his ears. Slim hung the lantern up on a nail, fetched a key from his pocket and unlocked the cell door. Oddly, he held no gun, although two six-shooters sagged low at his thighs.

"C'mon," said Slim.

Slowly Bide walked out of the cell. "What's up?" he asked, his eyes agate-cold on Slim's face.

"Yore brother," replied Slim, looking past him, "sent me to release yuh. Said he didn't want yuh to stay in the Gulch. It wasn't safe for yuh. Said he was doin' it for the Evans family."

For a brief instant Bide felt a warm glow go through him. Then it faded. The message was too obviously rehearsed. Slim was nervous, kept shifting his eyes, moving his hands near his thighs.

"Yeah," said Bide, with a show of relief. "That's mighty good of Matt. Where is he? I'd like to see him 'fore I go."

"He ain't here," Slim said hurriedly. "This way," he pointed to the rear door at the end of the corridor. "There's a hoss waitin' for yuh."

Bide started moving toward the door with Slim beside and to the rear of him, when he stopped and turned abruptly. He surprised a pale glitter in Slim's eyes.

"Forgot my Colts," said Bide. "They're in the office. I'll get 'em." He turned about and took one step toward the office door, when Slim's hand fell on his left arm.

"Yuh'll do without 'em," Slim cried shortly. "There ain't no time," he added. "It'll be sun-up soon."

Bide shrugged and nodded as though accepting the answer. But instead of turning back, suddenly pushed Slim aside with the latter's own hand. Then wheeling swiftly behind the gaunt claim-jumper, he slid his arm around Slim's neck until he had it locked in the crook of his elbow. Slim's hands pulled frantically at his circling arm.

He exerted sudden pressure and Slim began to choke. Snaking the claim-jumper's gun with his left hand, Bide released him, twisting him around as he did so.

"Stand hitched!" snapped Bide.

Slim's face was re l and he gasped for breath. His eyes glinted with anger as he looked into his own gun muzzle.

"What's the idea?" he cried finally. "Here I'm lettin' yuh out—and yuh go *loco*."

Bide relieved him of the other gun and then considered him through graying eyes. "Slim," he said, "maybe I'm

115

loco. But you and me are goin' to change places. Yuh're goin' out this way, and I'm leavin' by the front door. Oh—so yuh don't 'dmire that idea?"

A sudden change had swept Slim. The rage left his eyes —to be replaced by stark, abject fear. His mouth fell open and his lower lip trembled. He tried to speak, but no words came past his teeth. Finally, he shook his head.

"So yuh were goin' to send me out to be bushwhacked," muttered Bide grimly. "Then tomorrer the Gulch would say, 'Killed—tryin' to escape. Good riddance.' "

"It was Matt's idea," cried Slim fearfully.

"Matt?" said Bide, staring stonily at the other. Then, "Get back into the cell."

Willingly, the latter went into the cell Bide had occupied. Whipping off Slim's belt, Bide lashed the claim-jumper's hands behind his back and stuffed a handkerchief into his mouth. Then he went out and locked the door with the key.

He left the lantern hanging in the corridor and cautiously let himself into the office. Over in the east, a dull, gray morning of impending light came tenuously to the night. But outside the jail the inky pitch was still impenetrable.

The office was empty and Bide catfooted across the room. The front door creaked slightly as he opened it. Another sound reached him—the soft heave of horses. He placed them at the front left corner of the building.

Slowly he reached dust and then groped silently along the wall. His reaching hand suddenly touched horseflesh. Then a man close by cried out. Bide realized someone had been left to keep the horses quiet.

The Texan lashed out fiercely in the direction of the cry, and felt his fist make a pulpy sound as it connected with bone and flesh. Again the man cried out—this time loudly, stridently, his voice cleaving the darkness:

"This way! This way!"

Bide caught the bridle of the nearest horse and tried to get aboard, but the horse was nervous, kept plunging. Time was running out and the crunch of booted feet beating across the dirt rang menacingly in his ears.

Finally, desperately, he made leather and jabbed his spurs fast and deep. The animal lurched away at a dead run. Gunfire began to rattle in his ears. Gunfire and curses. Then the night seamed wide open in long scarlet splash-

116

es. Flaming muzzles cut jagged designs into the darkness. Blood suddenly ran warm down his arm as a bullet scored his shoulder. And the hot breath of death fanned his cheeks.

He let his horse run out the gauntlet of questing lead, crouching low in the saddle. Halfway down the main street, headed east, he looked back. Guns were still blazing yonder at the jail, and it looked like a Fourth of July celebration.

In a few moments he had made the other end of the town. Sliding off his mount, he went into the brush where he had left his black and pulled the horse out on the trail. There were no signs of pursuit, so he set a leisurely pace into the dawn-breaching sky.

The sun hatched out of its eastern shell with blood on it. It rose big and fiery—and hot before its time. The early morning earth had coolness along its banks, but that soon vanished in face of the raw-looking menace that hung over the ragged lip of the eastern fringe of hills like a bloody omen.

The morning matched Bide Evans' temper as he stomped the clearing at Dutch Diggings. Inside him there was something at work that seethed like a volcano. It set fire to his gray eyes and molded his jaw into a rough-hewn line.

"My own brother," he muttered. "Havin' me dry-gulched."

That, more than anything else, whipped him like a rawhide. All the bitterness of his six months' search returned. All his reasonings on Matt's possible innocence were wiped away. Matt was guilty as hell; and last night had proved it!

He was finished with doubts. From here on he moved in a single, straight line.

His thoughts shifted abruptly to Farrell and Ming. Black Henry had delegated two of his men to be at the diggings this morning. It was for these that Bide was waiting. They would lead him to Black Henry's hideout. Otherwise he might spend futile days combing these hills and gullies.

He hoped fervently he would be in time. He had seen an example of how Black Henry worked—and the sight hadn't been pleasant.

The distant crackling of twigs under the hoofs of a running horse came suddenly to his ears. He moved quickly behind a clump, where he had hidden his horse, and waited.

His forehead corrugated into a frown. Only one horse rode the approaching trail. Moreover, the animal was moving fast, with a hint of urgency in its fast-thudding hoofs. In a few moments a rider flashed into the clearing.

"Ming!" cried Bide, coming out of hiding.

Ming Foy's ordinarily placid, yellow face was a queer color with blood pumping into it. A great wave of relief swept it as he saw the Texan.

"Heaven smiles on Ming Foy," he cried excitedly. "You are here."

"Where's Ed?" asked Bide.

"In grave danger," replied Ming, briefly for once.

Bide Evans wheeled and went for his horse. Up in saddle he listened grimly to Ming's tale as they swung along.

"We got to get back there fast," Bide cried. "They'll take out their anger on Ed."

The bright-garbed Oriental brought his hand down hard on his mount's flank and the animal sped away. Bide followed on his heels, a streak of raw color in his face, his lean lips taut.

Along the base of the slope raced Ming, hunched in the saddle, his pigtail flying horizontally behind him. Ahead now, a short distance, lay his goal—the dense clump of trees that hid the ingress to the gorge. Speedily he made the fringe and then slowed his pace.

Carefully, he wound his way among the trees and shrubs. Bide, alongside Ming momentarily, caught sight of the entrance to the gorge through the brush. Abruptly he motioned Ming to halt. His narrowing eyes had seen a man on guard. The latter was seated, propped against a boulder, dozing. A rifle lay across his lap.

Slipping silently out of leather, Bide eased forward. Then warily he pulled up behind a tree—the last tree between him and the guard. In between them was a clear stretch of about twenty feet.

Gun palmed, the Texan stole softly across the rocky patch. Six feet from the nodding guard, the latter stirred uneasily. Bide stood rigid, held his breath. If the guard awoke he would give the alarm to the camp.

A warning signal must have clanged in the guard's brain, for his eyelids fluttered open suddenly. A low growl burst from his lips and he started to bring his rifle up.

118

Desperately, Bide Evans moved. In a single leap he lunged forward and brought his gun butt down hard on the man's twisting head. There was a sickening crunch as steel met bone—and the guard toppled and lay still.

Bide took the rifle and handed it to Ming, who came up on foot. "We'll have to leave the horses here," Bide told him, as he speedily bound and gagged the guard in the same manner he attended to Slim. "Can't take any chances on their hearin' us."

Ming gazed at the guard and shook his head. "This blot on nature," he said, "was not here before when I left."

Bide frowned. "That means there may be more than three of 'em there."

Quickly he passed along the narrow footing, picking his way among the large rocks and boulders. Ming followed nimbly behind. Then the defile spread out and Ming pointed to the brush tangle ahead.

But Bide needed no directions, for the ominous clump of a pickaxe biting into earth had reached his ears. With Ming at his heels he made the trees. He turned to the Chinese.

"Yuh stay put, Ming," he whispered. Then cautiously he began to circle the right flank of the clump. Hugging the protection of outhanging branches, Bide gradually worked his way around. A corral hove in sight. He thought he saw four horses. Actually there were five; but he didn't see the fifth because it was rolling at the time.

The edge of the cabin came into view. Then his lips pulled down in straight parallel lines. Ed Farrell stood there, swinging a pickaxe—digging another grave. Three men stood around watching. One Bide recognized as Pete, Slim's sidekick. Then he saw that his gray-haired friend had finished, so he pushed out from the brush, his guns leveled.

"Reach for that sky!" he cried sharply.

The three men whirled on him, then their hands fell away as they caught the deadly gleam of his Colts in the sun. They paled, recognizing him.

"Bide!" cried Ed Farrell, relief broad in his face. "Ming made it."

"Yeah," nodded Bide. "Take their hardware, Ed."

A smile washed the oldster's features and he began to pull their guns. Suddenly he let out a yell: "Bide! In the doorway!"

119

A gun blasted in the sunlight, and a triumphant yell rose from the cabin. Before the echo of the shot died away, another one, louder, more strident, beat across to the cabin. The yell there died suddenly, and the man holding a smoking gun in his hand abruptly collapsed in the center. His knees buckled and he pitched out on his face into the yard. He lay without moving and the mounting cries of the three outlaws fell away with his dying plunge.

Bide had turned at Ed's yell, but he was late. A hot stabbing pain seared through him as a bullet found his left shoulder. His eyes suddenly saw black and his stomach began to roll. For a second he thought he was going to pass out, and his hands felt weak and powerless. But with a wrench of will he pulled himself together—just in time to hear Ming's voice come gently from the other end of the tree clump:

"How are you, gentlemen?"

Then Bide saw him emerge with the rifle in his hands. A wisp of smoke lay wreathed around the muzzle.

18. *Showdown*

THE EARLY MORNING SUN glinted brightly from the star that Matt Evans wore on his vest. He cut his mount's pitching canter to a jog as he came into sight of the Gulch jailhouse.

He approached the building warily, his green eyes going to the three corners visible. Apparently satisfied that no one was lurking about, he drifted up and swung off his horse.

His clothes were rumpled, as though he had slept in them and his face was stubbled with a two days' growth. His guns shifted low against his thighs as he mounted the few steps and kicked the door in.

Hearing nothing, he entered, then closed the door with his boot. A sardonic smile came to his face as he passed the bulletin board.

"Mornin', Bide," he said to the Wanted poster there. He laughed briefly. "Reckon yuh'd be proud to know that yore lawman brother high-tailed on account of a pack of storekeepin' Vigilantes." He shook his head and he grimaced. "Sure makes me proud." He added, muttering, "Maybe I better change my name."

He frowned when he came to the door leading to the cell's corridor and found it slightly ajar. He considered it, then went past the door with hastening strides. Pulling up at the cell into which he had thrown his brother, he suddenly gave vent to a cry of surprise.

"Slim!" he roared. "What in hell are yuh doin' there? Where's my brother?"

But the gaunt claim-jumper was unable to answer. His mouth was stuffed with a red kerchief.

His lips flattened in a wolfish snarl, Matt feverishly unlocked the cell door and in a moment had the gag out of Slim's mouth.

"Well?" yelled the Gulch's lawman.

Slim breathed deeply, his sunken cheeks blowing in and out.

"Dang him," he cried finally. "Wurt told me to bring some food for him. So I did. When I get to the door, yore brother wraps his arm around my neck and takes my gun away. Then he shoves me in here."

Matt's green eyes burned hard into Slim's face, then he turned on his heel and crossed to the door. Slim's cry stopped him there.

"Hey! Ain't yuh goin' to let me out of here?"

Matt turned again. As he came back, his eyes swept the floor. Then something came into his face that was tough and bright—something that made his eyes glitter with a queer light.

"Slim," he said softly. "What kind of food did yuh bring him—with no plates?"

Slim's eyes widened, and fear rode into them. He stepped backward to the wall as Matt advanced on him.

"Yuh danged liar!" Matt yelled. He reached out and seized Slim by the throat. Rage gripped the tin-starred, redheaded man and he shook his prisoner savagely. Slim's face grew red, purple, black. Finally Matt loosened his stranglehold.

Gradually the colors faded away from the gaunt man's face. He gulped air into his mouth in deep sobs. Between panting breaths he told Matt what had happened. "He forgot about me—Wurt did, dang him!" Slim concluded.

For an instant Matt glared at him, then with set teeth let go and drove his balled fist, hard and clean into Slim's mouth. There was a sharp smack; then Matt wheeled out of the cell, not waiting to see Slim sag to the floor.

Matt Evans went through the office looking neither to the right nor left. A murderous expression was building up in his face. When he hit the yard he was running and he went up into saddle with a savage kick.

"Playin' me for a sucker, huh?" he bit out through clenched teeth.

In a moment his mount was racing down the Gulch's main street, a swirling dust streamer, yellow in the morning sun raising in its wake. The1 the animal went back on its haunches and reared as Matt pulled the reins sharply in front of the Star.

He was off the horse and pushing through the batwings before the animal quieted. The saloon was virtually empty, except for one or two drunks sprawled in chairs. The baggy-eyed bartender, polishing the mahogany bar, looked up.

"Howdy, Matt," he called.

"Highpockets," said Matt, "where's Jim?"

"Upstairs—in his room," replied the bartender, half-smiling, half-dubious. He wrinkled his sallow face and scratched his head as he saw the sheriff go up the stairs three at a time. "Kind of in a hurry, I reckon."

Matt reached the landing and whirled down the open corridor. Then without knocking, he went into Jim Wurt's room.

Jim Wurt was putting the finishing touches on his morning's dress; combing his hair and smoothing his mustache. The owner of the Star raised his eyebrows at the abrupt entrance. Then something in his visitor's face caused the blood to wash out of Wurt's high forehead; made him move back a step.

"Howdy, Matt," he said, his voice ragged around the edges.

Matt stared at him, his wide chest rising and falling rapidly. Then words chopped out of his mouth in short, spaced intervals.

"Wurt," he said. "I'm goin' to give yuh the worst beatin' yuh ever got in yore life."

If there was any blood left in Wurt's face it went away

now. Fear came fresh to his eyes, and his chin seemed to tremble.

"Yuh're *loco,* Matt," he cried, taking another step backward.

"No," grunted Matt. "But I been blind *loco* up to now."

"What are yuh talkin' about?" cried Wurt.

"Send me out on a wild-goose chase—huh!" Matt cried, his eyes narrowed to green pin-points. "So yuh could get Bide. Yuh sent him three of the boys, all right. And last night yuh sent all of 'em—huh? But he got away—didn't he? Maybe yuh could fool one Evans—but not two—huh Wurt?"

"Yuh're *loco,* Matt," repeated Wurt, pantingly. His tongue was out, licking his full red lips. He was a smallish man compared to Matt, but now he seemed to grow smaller, to shrink.

"Yeah," continued Matt slowly, disregarding the interruption. His eyes were glued to Wurt's smooth-shaven face. "It was Bide yuh was out for since he got here. And why?" He paused and his lips went back over his teeth.

"Yuh're wrong, Matt," cried Wurt. "Yuh're wrong!"

"Sure," Matt went on relentlessly. "Cause Bide suspected Abe Symes was alive when I left the bank that night. Yuh were afeared, Wurt, 'cause yuh knew Symes was alive. I let yuh talk me out of rememberin' I lost the gold charm at yore place—didn't I? And I let yuh feed me whiskey so's I'd forget. So's I'd forget the steamin' hoss I saw in front of yore place that night. The hoss that was in back of the bank. So's I'd forget to ask yuh who yuh suddenly won the money from to buy a saloon—huh?"

Wurt was back now against the wall and the truth lay bare in his bloodless face.

Matt went on, his rage a temporarily controlled volcano. "But yuh slipped up, friend. Yuh got careless. Maybe yuh wasn't in Dudley long enough to find out Symes' right arm was paralyzed—huh? So yuh pinned it on me 'cause everyone would believe it. Yuh framed me, Wurt—friend!" He spat the last into Wurt's face. And then his arms went flashing back as Wurt fumbled at his sleeve.

"Go ahead, Jim," Matt called tauntingly. "I ought to drill yuh 'thout waitin' for yore draw. But I never shot a man down in cold blood—and I ain't goin' to start on a skunk like yuh."

Wurt dropped his hands to his sides. "I was wrong, Matt," he pleaded. "I tried to make it up for yuh by gettin' yuh elected sheriff."

"Yuh're a liar!" cried Matt. "Yuh got me elected 'cause yuh wanted to run this town. But this is yore last day in the Gulch, Mr. Wurt. Yuh're goin' to sign a confession to the murder of Abe Symes, and take yore beatin'."

"I ain't signin' nothin'!" snapped Wurt.

He had overstepped himself. A wicked grin tore across Matt's face and he drawled, "Them's the words I 'dmire to hear, friend." He moved slowly across the room.

Downstairs, at the bar, Highpockets suddenly stopped shining his glassware and cocked an ear. Over his head, the floor began to shake. And the back bar mirror started to quiver.

He screwed his eyes up and listened intently. "Sounds like a fuss," he muttered dubiously. "In Wurt's room, too." His angled shoulders moved in a shrug.

For a while, the scuffling, smacking sounds overhead went on unabated. Several times there was a sudden, heavy noise, as of something falling. Highpockets shook his head perplexedly. There was a short space of time when all noise ceased, except a kind of sighing wheeze.

The high-built bartender sighed too; but even as he was releasing his breath the sounds above started all over again. But now their duration was brief. There was a sudden crash and then a scraping, as if a body were being dragged across the floor. But that was impossible, Highpockets knew.

Complete silence now reigned, so the bartender went back to work. He was so engaged when Matt Evans came sauntering down the stairs. The sheriff, he noted, was folding a piece of paper with a highly pleased look on his face.

"Set one up for me," called the latter. He came over with a light step and wide grin and tossed the drink off in a gulp. "On the house, Highpockets," said the sheriff. And he turned and walked out of the saloon.

The bartender stared after Matt Evans and scratched his head. He had never seen Evans acting coltish. Matt had always been the morose kind.

Painfully, Jim Wurt dragged himself across the floor to the dresser. With great effort he propped himself up and stared into the mirror. He groaned aloud. His face was smeared with blood that streamed from his nose. Red bruises, where Matt's knuckles left their marks, showed up high and puffy on his cheekbones. His lower lip was cut and his white shirt was blood-spattered and dirty. Only his eyes had somehow escaped damage. And now they glared back at him balefully, full of a burning, lustful hatred.

"Damn yuh!" His voice was hoarse and his words a croak. "Damn yuh, Matt Evans! Both of yuh!"

He left the dresser, made it across the room to where a filled washbowl stood on a small table, and staggered back with it. With a towel he washed his bruises. The water burned his face and he grimaced into the mirror.

In a couple minutes, he wobbled to the door and holding on to the frame, called down for a bottle. When Highpockets came up, he thrust his hand through the slightly opened door and took the bottle from him.

"Is Black Henry still here?" Wurt put his voice through the wedge.

"Think so," returned Highpockets from the outside.

"Send him up," ordered Wurt thickly and closed the door. He quickly tilted the bottle and let the liquor trickle down past his swollen tongue to his throat. Wurt was not a drinker, but this made him feel better. He took a second swig and the whiskey began to burn him. He shook his fist at the door.

"I ain't leavin' town, Matt Evans," he cried, a sudden mad glint in his eye. " 'Cause yuh're leavin' first—by way of Dud Harvey's." His voice cracked, split shrill. "And I'll buy yuh the best box he's got, Matt. The best one! That's because I'm a good friend of yores. Ha! ha! Maybe I'll buy yuh two. Sure—yore brother'll need one also."

He took one more drink. He put the bottle away from him. The hectic flush receded from his face, the fever left his eye, and he calmed. Jim Wurt had had his ups and downs, and knew the value of a coldly sober head. And, for what he had in mind, he would need a cool brain.

Outside of the marks on his face, Jim Wurt was a well-tailored man when Black Henry came into the room. His black hair was carefully brushed, his mustache shiny with bear grease, his white linen shirt spotless.

"By the great horn spoon!" cried Black Henry, catching sight of Wurt's face. "What happened to yuh?"

125

"Matt let the star on his vest go to his head," said Wurt curtly. "He's feelin' righteous—and he's cleanin' up the town. He started on me." His voice broke as he put a hand to his face. "Blast him!" But it was momentary and his voice fell even again. "He told me to hit the trail."

"Why the ungrateful son!" roared Black Henry. "Yuh make him sheriff, and he wants to run yuh out of town. Why—it ain't natural!"

"He told me yuh're next on the list," Wurt said calmly. "Yuh and the Hounds."

The thick-chested man broke into a round of profanity. His fox eyes grew small and his pocked face red. He wound up with: "I'll go get that son now," and started for the door.

Wurt halted him. "Wait," he said. "I got other plans first. I think maybe we'll leave the Gulch anyhow. 'Cause when we get through here there won't be much of a town left."

"What do yuh mean?" demanded the huge man.

Wurt told him briefly, succinctly, and his black eyes glittered with a strange light as he wove his web of death and destruction.

Black Henry listened carefully, his eyes roving the room. His gaze came to rest and stayed in the far corner where a trunk lay with some clothes piled on the top.

"What about the Vigilantes?" he asked.

"They're lost without Larson," replied Wurt. "And I can handle 'em now."

"And my cut?" asked Black Henry quietly.

"The same."

The heavy-set man shook his head. "No," he said.

"We have an agreement," declared Wurt.

"Times change," said Black Henry, rising. "The boys are complainin'." He crossed the room casually to the trunk, poked his finger among the clothes and came up with a red wig. He gazed quizzically at Wurt. "Thought I heard somethin' about Larson's killer bein' redheaded?" He screwed his eyes, and then as an afterthought: "Safe cleaned out, too."

Fresh blood whipped into Wurt's cheeks, and he glared fiercely at Black Henry. Then his gaze fell against the other's growing smile.

"All right," he said. "Fifty-fifty."

"On Larson's gold too?"

"Yeah." The word was wrenched out of Wurt.

"See yuh tonight, pard," said Black Henry. He came back across the room, dropped the wig into Wurt's hand and went out the door.

Wurt ground his teeth, slammed the wig to the floor, stamped on it with both his feet, and kicked it away from him. It slid along the floor like a leaf in a gust of wind, and came to rest under the bed.

19. The Red Wig

THE RIDE back to Dutch Diggings was a dim and painful memory to Bide Evans. Every stride of the horse sent a jarring pain stabbing through his shoulder. It seemed to swell, grow larger; then throb like the pulsating artery in his throat.

The pounding reached his head and set an anvil clanging there. It became a deafening roar in his ears. His stomach gripped with bitter nausea, and sheer agony fluttered at his eyes.

He grew dizzy and would have fallen several times but for the arm Farrell threw about him. Remotely, the anxious voice of the oldster reached him.

"Easy, Bide," called Farrell. "We'll be there soon and Ming'll get to work on yuh. He's a genuine doctor."

His smile was a grimace of pain and words formed on his lips, but he heard no sound of them. It seemed days before he finally reached the lean-to at Dutch Diggings.

For a time, the world eddied around him, then things cleared and he found Ming bending over him. The latter was holding a cup to his lips.

Farrell stood at Ming's shoulder, nodding his grayed head.

"Drink it, Bide," he said. "Do yuh good. Ming's own brew."

Bide drank it down. It left a deep, bitter taste in his mouth. It took effect almost immediately and he felt as if he were floating.

127

He saw Ming make preparations to remove the bullet. A fire was built, clean strips of cloth prepared and the small, sharp knife played over the fire. Deftly, Ming went probing for the lead pellet.

A momentary twinge shot through Bide's shoulder, and then the bullet was out. Quickly Ming washed and cleansed the wound, bandaged it and then gave him another cup of the bitter brew to drink. Bide was on the point of saying something, forgot what it was, and fell asleep.

When he woke, the sun was making a red-rusty splash of color over to the west. He jumped to his feet, something urgent pressing him, then almost staggered back.

"Heck!" he muttered. "Forgot I had a bum shoulder."

A sharp, clean pain went through the shoulder as he steadied himself. But he found his legs firm and discovered as he walked to the door, that if he carried the wounded shoulder a trifle higher than the other, there would be almost no pain at all.

Farrell, carrying two filled buckets down to the stream's edge where Ming sat at the rocker, caught sight of him and let out a yell:

"Hey! Get back to the bunk."

Bide smiled faintly, shook his head, "I'm all right, Ed," he declared. "Doctor Foy fixed me up good."

"Yeah," argued the oldster, setting down his buckets. "But yuh shouldn't be up yet."

Instead of answering, Bide brought out the question that must have lain in his mind while he slept, for he woke with it on his tongue. "What did yuh learn back there, Ed?" He already knew part of the answer.

"Plenty," cried Farrell. Briefly, he told Bide what he heard at the cabin. That Black Henry, Jim Wurt and Matt Evans were linked together in a claim-jumping outfit. That Jim Wurt was the "brains" behind the organization and the latter was going to give Black Henry and the Hounds the word to move into the Gulch in a day or two. "And," he continued, "that it was yore brother's picture on the Wanted poster—not yores."

"Yeah," muttered Bide grimly. "But leave that to me. It sure looks like hell's goin' to pop soon."

"Maybe sooner," said Farrell.

Bide said, "What do yuh mean?"

"Miner come out of town down the stream this after-

128

noon," Farrell replied. "Asked me if I wanted to buy a saloon. Said the Star was for sale."

"It's tonight!" cried Bide, foreboding strong in him. "Whatever's goin' to happen, will be tonight."

"What's the diff'rence?" demanded the oldster. "Don't matter to us."

Bide said slowly: "I think it does, Ed. Saddle up for me, will yuh?"

"Yuh're *loco*," cried Farrell. "Yuh can't ride with that shoulder."

Bide shook his head. Farrell argued it a minute, but he found the Texan adamant, and finally gave in. In a short while three horses stood saddled.

" 'Bout time we paid the Gulch a visit—huh, Ming?" said Farrell. "Good thing we borrered two hosses this mornin'. How does she feel, Bide?"

As Bide climbed awkwardly into his saddle, pain raked him. He grunted, "All right." But as he headed the black down the trail with his two friends bringing up the rear, his shoulder gave him plenty of trouble. He set his teeth and by riding the stirrups found he could make the pain bearable.

He could think of nothing else as he rode through the accumulating gloom. Complete darkness fell before he finally saw the flares set into the main street of the Gulch. Then he got down and walked the rest of the way.

There was a roaring, drinking crowd filling the town this night, Bide saw, and he nodded. He knew that he and his friends would be watched for—they were too dangerous on the loose for Wurt and his gang.

"Ed," he said to the gray-hair beside him, "yuh and Ming find Tay Brown or Dan Rivers and tell 'em to warn the Vigilantes—'cept about Matt. I'll see him. Tell 'em to be on the close watch tonight. And after yuh find 'em— meet me in front of Larson's. Hurry."

He saw them angle across the street and disappear into the crowd. Then he walked quickly down the left-hand side of the street, and pulled up at a darkened warehouse, three buildings from the Star.

With a quick glance around to see if he was observed, Bide sidled into the darkened alley of the warehouse, pulling his black behind. No light from the street reached to the back of the building, but a moon was coming up.

129

It gave enough light to permit the Texan to move without crashing into water barrels.

The pain was beginning to run his left side. Then he reached the back shed of the Star. It was harder this time to get up into saddle and the sweat started under his wide-brim before he made it. He sat a minute letting breath pull in and out of his chest. Then, with his hand on the end pole of the shed to steady him, he climbed to his feet on slippery leather.

His head and shoulder came up above the shed, and the rising moon glinted back at him from the row of lightless windows at the upper end of the shed's slope.

Grasping the rough edge, he slowly began to haul himself up. Pain worked him in earnest now. Sweat covered his back, glued his shirt tight. Hot tears of agony blinded him. He bit his lip and felt the warm blood spurt into his mouth.

Finally he made it, and lay gasping on the shed's roof. He spewed out the blood and felt the rough shingles rasp his cheek. He sprawled there until the wave of pain receded.

Slowly, carefully, he moved up the slanting roof. He had firmly fixed in his mind the night before, the room from which Wurt had emerged.

Reaching it, he raised the window cautiously, and stepped into the room. The strengthening light of the moon filled the place; and a yellow streak came from under the door.

"Looks like movin' day," Bide muttered.

The room lay disheveled, clothes strewn on the floor. An open trunk sat in the corner, piled high with odds and ends of stuff. Quickly, Bide went over there and began emptying it.

He was down on his knees. It eased his shoulder that way; and he kept reaching into the trunk. A crack in the dresser mirror caught a light beam and threw it in his face. It showed building disappointment.

He was down at the bottom when his hand touched something damp. He hauled up with it and came fast to the window. It was a wet miner's coat. His eyes filled with a cold, gray light as the moon showed a clean rip, near the pocket.

Bide laid the coat aside and went scouting around the

130

room. He pulled the two dresser drawers and emptied them on the floor.

He shook his head. "Not here," he muttered. "Can't be half-right. Or maybe Charlie Oaks was dreamin' up that actin' troupe with the impersonator?"

He circled the room again, unmindful of the pulsing fire in his shoulder. Sounds from the saloon below seeped through the walls, but he paid them no attention. The circle he made became narrower. Finally, pulling up in the center of the room, he kicked a red-spattered shirt aside in expasperation.

Suddenly his eye hooked on something beneath the bed. Kneeling quickly, he thrust his hand underneath—and came up with a red wig.

He started for the window. A flood of light sprang suddenly into the room as the door flung open—and caught him squarely in its center. A yell burst from the man at the door.

Wheeling, Bide's good arm flashed back in a blur of speed and plucked his gun from holster.

"Shut up, Wurt!" he cried. "And get in here."

But Wurt remained there, a contorted smile on his face.

"It won't do yuh no good, Bide Evans," he cried. "The place is surrounded. Yuh were seen comin'."

Quickly, Bide backed to the window and cast a downward glance. Shadowy forms of men were moving there.

"So a redheaded killer done in Larson?" he cried, coming up to Wurt and waving the wig in his face.

The latter stood his ground, and laughed hoarsely. "Yeah," he yelled. "Sure it was me. So what?"

"This!" clipped Bide, stuffing the wig into his pocket and jabbing the Colt's muzzle into Wurt's ribs. "Yuh and me are goin' out the front door together. The Vigilantes will be glad to see yuh."

Fear flooded Wurt's face momentarily, then he sneered and laughed again. "Yuh won't get out," he said. "My boys won't let yuh."

"We'll see!" cried Bide grimly. "Get movin'."

He pushed Wurt ahead of him slowly along the open corridor that ran over the bar.

"He's here, boys!" shouted Wurt loudly, suddenly.

A sharp abrupt silence fell over the crowd as they lifted their eyes and watched the two men overhead.

Eyes narrowed to thin slits, Bide sized them warily; he took Wurt to the landing and started moving down the stairway.

"By the great horn spoon!" gasped someone in a far corner. "The gent's got his nerve!"

But silence swallowed the sound of his words and clamped down hard over the tense and breathless room. Bide felt it press against him; felt Wurt sending frantic signals out with his eyes.

He reached the foot of the stairs and began to work his way toward the door. His back suddenly felt chilly. Pressure was building up in the room, expanding. Abruptly it broke open to the jammer of six guns in action. Shouts, wild screams filled the air as lead shattered the hanging lamps and plunged the saloon into darkness.

Swiftly, Bide clouted Wurt on the head with the Colt butt. Wurt slumped to the floor and Bide, jamming his gun back into holster, leaped over his body and made for the door.

Stooping low he ran, and gun muzzles cut brief orange patterns at him across the pitch-black depths. A big, shapeless mass of flesh tangled his way. Desperately Bide ground his fists into the man's belly. There was a grunt of pain and the circling arms fell away.

Stabbing agony knifed through the Texan and he felt sticky warmth spread over his shoulder. As he crashed through to the doors, he realized that his shoulder wound had opened. Already his shirt was wet.

He fought back the faintness that threatened to overwhelm him and came out running. He caught sight of Farrell and Ming reining over from the other side of the street, and then he made the leather of a horse standing at the high post, in a last burst of strength.

"C'mon!" he yelled at them and sent his mount whirling down the street. They spurred after him quickly. Over his shoulder he saw men burst out of the saloon, shooting, yelling; then climb their horses and set out in hot pursuit.

He was rapidly growing weaker from loss of blood. He waved Farrell and Ming ahead of him and yelled at them, "Keep movin'," threw a couple of shots at his pursuers to slow them up—and went flying off his horse.

He landed on his feet, but the momentum hurled him forward into the garden bed of a house near the end of the town. He crashed into some shadowy bushes and lay

132

still. Faintly he heard the drum of hoofbeats and rumble of gunfire pass him by. Then all became quiet.

A light fell suddenly athwart his back. Slowly he turned over and saw the door of the house had opened. A girl stood in the doorway—Kate Larson, with a rifle in her hands. He lurched to his feet, stood swaying, staring at her.

For an instant, terror filled her eyes, then anger blazed through with recognition.

"You!" she cried. She pointed her rifle at him, fresh blood pumping to her face.

He smiled, but realized it was a foolish smile, for he had momentarily lost control of his face muscles. "Sorry, Kate," he mumbled. "Smashed yore garden."

"Murderer!" she cried at him.

He shook his head wearily. "Mistake," he mumbled, his tongue thick. "Mistake."

He felt her eyes on his face, dark and piercing, probing his heart, searching his soul. Then something came to her lovely face, touched it, lightened it. Slowly, her breast heaving, she lowered the rifle.

"That's what—" she began, then she saw his shoulder. "You're wounded," she cried.

She came quickly from the doorway and helped him into the house. He leaned upon her and felt her warm and alive against him.

He slumped into a chair and watched her face as she cut his shirt open and brought basin and bandages. Her motions were fast, efficient as she washed his shoulder.

He spoke, but his tongue was addled and his voice sounded far away. "I'm takin' yuh back to Texas with me, Kate," he said.

Blood stained her face. "Be quiet," she said sharply. "You're feverish."

He shook his head. "Mind's clear as a bell," he protested weakly. Her eyes were intent on the bandages. "Yuh'll like Texas, Kate. Grass for miles, the plains as big as the sky, bellowin' longhorns—yuh'll like it."

He couldn't see her face, for she was carrying the basin away. When she came back, slim-waisted, graceful, hazel eyes steady, he could read nothing there.

"It was you wearing the sheriff's badge last night in the store?" she asked suddenly. "Wasn't it?"

"Our spread stretches for miles and miles," he answered

softly. "Take yuh eight days to ride from one end to the other."

"Your eyes were gray," she said. "And I remembered the scar on your neck." She touched his neck lightly.

" 'Course," he said, his tongue growing thicker, "I can't be home all the time—'specially durin' round-up. And maybe have to take a herd across the nations—"

Kate Larson had a faraway look in her face and her red curving lips were parted slightly. She brought her eyes around to him, and even in his addled state, he could feel the shock.

"Do both your father's sons drink, Bide?" she asked softly.

20. *Favor for a Favor*

BEFORE KATE'S meaning came home to him, the clatter of horses suddenly rumbled up out of the night. Bide barely had time to turn, when the door burst open. Masked, armed men crowded into the room.

"All right, Bide Evans," cried the leader, in a voice unfamiliar to Bide. "C'mon. Don't be alarmed, Miss Larson. No harm will come to yuh."

"What are you going to do with him?" Kate cried, concern in her voice, in her eyes.

"The Vigilantes will give him a fair trial, ma'm," said the leader.

Then two men pulled Bide to his feet, took his guns away and tied his hands behind his back. They hustled him to the door. A kind of paralysis held Bide, shaken only by the renewed pain in his shoulder.

He was hauled outside, searched and pushed up on a horse. The cool night air brushed away some of the cobwebs in his brain.

His mount moved with the rest. Then they pulled up at the jailhouse and another group of masked men joined them.

"Well?" demanded the leader.

"He ain't here," answered the one addressed. There

was disappointment in his voice. "Must've flew the coop."

"We got one of 'em," said the leader.

Suddenly Bide's eyes widened. His two friends, Farrell and Ming, sat there among the second group—bound and gagged.

"Hey," he cried. "What do yuh want with them two? They've done nothin'."

"Shut up!" shouted the leader.

A sense of something wrong, outside of his own predicament, came to Bide. If Ed and Ming had warned the Vigilantes, why were they prisoners? His captors had called him, "Bide Evans"; there was no mistake this time.

Then one group headed back to town, but left the gray-haired miner and his Chinese partner behind. Now they drifted up to the first tree span this side of the jail and halted. The masked men got off their horses, stuck a few flares into the earth and lighted them. And then under a low, outstretched limb of an oak, they were fixing ropes. A chill, not of the night, touched Bide.

"What was that word about a trial I was supposed to get?" he demanded.

The leader laughed roughly. "This is the only trial yuh're gettin', Evans—yuh and yore two pals."

The men handling the ropes had finished. Now, three lengths of rawhide with loops at their ends, hung silently next to each other from the branch.

Dryness parched Bide's mouth, and his shoulder got worse. He had known that one day the inevitable would occur, but he hardly fancied this method of making his exit. Moreover, there was a girl with hazel eyes—

"Walk their hosses under the trees," cried the leader. "C'mon now. We ain't got all night. We got important business."

The masked man alongside Bide pushed his mount forward. Bide caught Farrell's face in the flarelight. It was pale, but resigned. Ming's face and eyes were absolutely unreadable.

A clear unexpected voice broke over the hanging party.

"Get 'em lifted, gents."

A gasp of surprise was wrenched from underneath several masks as the riders wheeled and went clawing for their guns.

Crash!

A six-shooter roared and a masked rider cried out in

135

brief torment, dropped the gun he pulled and slumped across the horse's neck. The horse reared and the rider slipped out of saddle. He lay still.

"Get 'em lifted, gents," the same voice drawled—and now they did. The newcomer drifted into the lighted area ahorse. Apparently he had been hiding in the nearby brush. The flares gleamed in the star pinned to his vest.

"Matt," cried Bide.

"Howdy, Bide," said his brother. "Favor for a favor. Move up, I'll cut yuh loose."

Frowning, Bide kicked his horse over to his brother, turned and felt a knife cleave through his bonds. His shoulder was beginning to work a sweat through him and he started to get dizzy again. But he took the knife from his brother and set Farrell and Ming free. The latter two went among the riders and took their guns.

"Have a look under their masks, Matt," said Bide, eyeing the masked leader.

"Don't try it," cried the masked leader.

"That's an invitation," said Matt grinning. "Is yores comin' off or do I have to shoot it off?"

The leader shook his head stubbornly. His hat suddenly blew off his head, and then came the report of Matt's gun.

Trembling, the leader now raised unsteady fingers and took off his mask. He was a wide-lipped, squat man. Rumbling hoof thuds abruptly beat across to them from the west. Apprehensively, the masked men looked at each other.

"All right, Lippy," Matt told the leader. "Start movin' that way. All of yuh." He pointed his gun in the direction of the oncoming horses. *"Pronto."* To help them along, he put a couple of shots at their horses' legs.

Bide started to say something, but the chills had turned to fever, his head grew hot and heavy, and then things went suddenly black before him.

Later, Bide regained a fevered consciousness. He frowned, trying to remember where he was. Farrell's voice cut through his daze.

"Brother brought yuh to the jug," he heard the latter say.

Another question struggled to Bide's mind. "The Vigilantes," he said weakly. "Did yuh tell 'em?"

"Couldn't find 'em," replied Farrell. "Someone sent 'em on a wild goose chase. But I think it was the Vigilantes yore brother sent them masked hellions backin' into. We was in here by then."

"Where's Matt?" asked Bide. His voice sounded faint in his ears.

"Went out," answered the oldster. "Left a note for yuh. I'll put it in yore pocket," Farrell's voice was remote. It went on: "Yuh'll read it in the mornin'. Ming," the gray-haired man apparently turned to his partner close by, "give Bide another swig of that brew yuh brought along."

The yellowish, oriental face of Ming Foy swung before Bide and then a bottle was put to his lips. The taste was bitter to his tongue; then his eyes grew heavy and he drifted off into a deep sleep.

Faint sounds of gunfire, followed by a crash, roused Bide. Bright sunlight lay across his bunk, and he blinked as he opened his eyes.

"Where the heck am I?" he muttered, pushing up from his bed. Swift pain reminded him; and with a sudden rush, all the hazy memories of the past night swept before him. Through the bars of the adjoining cell he could see the two partners still asleep.

He struggled up despite the pain, swung off the bunk, took three steps toward the open cell door; and then his knees almost buckled. He realized that although his fever was gone, he was still plenty weak. He moved back to his bunk wondering about the gunfire and crash and sat down. Then he recalled the note that Farrell stuffed into his pocket. His hands fumbled for it, then found it.

Before he had a chance to read it, he heard the sudden, rapid drumbeat of hoofs on turf away from the jail. He turned and looked out of the window. Cold hackles rose on the back of his neck.

"Wurt and Black Henry!" he cried.

A grim foreboding rankled through him and he looked abstractly at the note in his hand. Its meaning sank slowly into his mind. Then he left the bunk like an uncoiling spring, whipping anger giving new energy to his limbs.

"Matt!" he cried, hauling through the cell door. "They got Matt." As he wheeled down the corridor, he caught Farrell and Ming stirring. Plunging past the office door, he pulled up abruptly, his fears confirmed.

His brother lay prone on the floor, two fresh pools of blood forming near him. He kneeled down beside Matt,

137

his own pain forgotten; his face grim, his eyes green with Arctic cold.

For a minute he thought his brother was done for. Then Matt stirred and his eyes fluttered open.

There was great pain in them, and Matt's lips flattened back against his teeth. His voice was hoarse and low.

"Them two skunks done for me, Bide," Matt gritted out. "When my back was turned." His face muscles contorted.

"I'm sorry, Matt," cried Bide, the blood gone from his face. That covered everything. His harshness to Matt, his pride, his obstinacy, his mistakes. Everything.

"Thanks, Bide," breathed Matt. "They burned half the town down last night and looted it." Then, slowly, "Yuh can do somethin' for me—" His voice petered out, his eyes closed, his breathing became inaudible.

"Sure," cried Bide hoarsely. "What is it, Matt?"

Matt wet his lips and his hand groped up to his vest. With great difficulty he unpinned the star.

"Take it," he said, "and show 'em the kind of sheriff an Evans can be."

Tears came unashamed to Bide's eyes. He took the badge and pinned it to his vest. "Favor for a favor, brother," he said softly. "I'm goin' to show 'em the kind of sheriff Matt Evans could be."

Warmth turned the green light gray in Matt's eyes a moment. "Thanks, Bide." Then the warmth abruptly left them. And Matt turned his face away, and died.

For a brief moment, Bide remained kneeling at Matt's side. Then he took his brother's Colts and arose. Farrell and Ming were standing quietly at the corridor. Without a word to them, he left the jail office.

There was a tight, constricted feeling in his throat as he went up onto Matt's horse and sent him along the main street. There was a hardness and toughness in him now that could only be resolved by vengeance, by the splitting roar of guns.

His eyes were wary as they went along the sides of the street. But they barely noticed the desolate, charred half of the town. Then he found what he was looking for. Two horses made a pair in front of the Star.

He left leather and went up the porch steps with a stiffened stride. A gust of coarse, familiar laughter swept through the batwings. Then he was past them.

"Black Henry," he called to the huge man at the bar. "Turn around and take yore call from Matt Evans."

Slowly, as though he had not heard right, the black-bearded man turned. His fox-eyes opened wide.

"Matt!" he cried hoarsely.

"Start workin'," cried Bide coldly. "This is goin' to be a mite harder than gettin' me in the back. Draw, damn yuh!"

"Matt!" Black Henry cried, unbelieving. Then, abruptly, his elbows faded backward. His body was away from the bar, his feet planted wide, his right shoulder slightly hunched from the draw. And that's the way he was standing when Bide Evans' bullets crashed against his chest.

The shots echoed through an empty saloon, for Bide was already wheeling out through the swinging doors. The sight of the big man suddenly growing rigid, then buckling and fading down into the sawdust, was already a memory.

Across the street he strode, making for "Sam Larson's General Store." Then he pulled short. Jim Wurt had come flying out of the store, apparently having heard the shots. The smaller man went dead white at the sight of the lean, starred figure.

"Matt?" His voice cracked high, wavered, fell.

"That's right, Jim," Bide said softly."And I'm arrestin' yuh for the murder of Sam Larson—and Abe Symes."

Desperation was in Wurt. It showed in the frantic way he pulled the derringer from his sleeve holster.

Coolly, Bide placed a shot into Wurt's arm. The derringer flew to the street. Wurt cried out in pain—and fear.

Dan Rivers came blinking out of his store. "What's goin' on?" he called.

"Rivers," said Bide sharply. "I'm deputizin' yuh here and now. Take the prisoner—" he wagged his gun at Wurt, "to jail."

"Yuh bet," cried Rivers, coming over.

Bide said, "Murdered Larson." He handed the printer his gun and went up the steps past Wurt.

Rivers steadied the gun against Wurt, shaking his head. "Complete change in the man," he murmured. "Beats everythin'. Almost cleaned up the Hounds single-handed last night—till the Committee came back. And now—c'mon, Wurt." He watched the latter move down dejectedly.

"We were lookin' for yuh, mister," he said. "One of yore friends confessed last night. Smart scheme keepin' a man at the claims office to copy down all the new claims entered—and then sendin' Black Henry to jump 'em. Very smart. Come on, now."

Kate Larson was moving toward the door when she stopped short, her face suddenly white. Her eyes went from the badge to Bide Evans' face, and eyes.

"I been tryin' to get a box of cartridges—for a .45 Colt, ever since I came to the Gulch," he began.

"Bide!" Kate cried, the blood pulsing back to her cheeks, her lips parting.

Then the two of them met in the middle of the empty store. His arms went around her shoulders, crushed her to him; then his lips were down on hers, bruising, hard. The world swam and tossed about them.

Laughing, her eyes wide and starry, Kate pushed away after a while.

"I didn't hear the answer to the question I asked last night," she said.

Once more he pulled her toward him. "Does it make any difference?"

"No," she said, and surrendered eagerly to his hungry embrace.

Two weeks later, Dan Rivers stood in the doorway of his printing shop and watched the forms of Hangman's Gulch's recently resigned sheriff and his pretty bride, the former Kate Larson, fade down the street. He took his stub of a pencil from behind his ear and fooled with it. Then with an air of perplexity, he turned to his son Bud, and said:

"Somethin' mighty funny 'bout that gent Evans, Bud. Could have sworn he was Bide, yet he kept sayin' he was Matt, and that the one they buried was Bide. Farrell and his partner kept callin' him both. Kate slipped up and called him 'Bide' yesterday. Then, he wanted to pay me again for bustin' up the place. Mighty queer, I call it. Somethin' very funny, bout that gent Evans."

"Maybe he's both, Dad," suggested Bud, brightly. "Say, whatever happened to the gold Wurt took out of Larson's safe?"

"I'm holdin' that information for the next edition, Bud," said Rivers.

"What happened to it?" insisted the youngster.

"Well, if yuh can keep a secret—for more than two minutes," declared his father, "I'll tell yuh. Yuh know what happened when Farrell's claim petered out?"

"Sure," cried Bud. "He and Ming Foy bought the general store from Miss Larson."

"That's right," nodded the hulking printer. "Ming found the gold in the back room, stuffed under a coffee bag. Wurt was comin' back to get it that mornin'."

"Here comes the new sheriff, Dad," said the youngster.

Rivers turned to the dark-faced man who was coming up. "Howdy, Brown," he said.

THE END